I'd rather glue me nut sack to a bullet train

HETTIE ASHWIN

Published by Slipperygrip 2019

I'd rather glue me nut sack to a bullet train.

ISBN: 978-2-9566868-0-4

Slipperygrip11@gmail.com

Books by Hettie Ashwin

Humour

Literary Licence

The Reluctant Messiah

Mr Tripp buys a lifestyle

Barney's Test

The Truffle War

Fat Bits

Boat to Baguette

Murder! Mayhem! and lesser cuts of meat.

Thriller

The Crowing of the Beast

The Mask of Deceit

Short Stories

After the Rains & other Stories

A shilling on the Bar

www.hettieashwin.blogspot.com.au

He's me mate

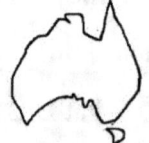

It all started with a telephone call. Not that a telephone call is something to remark upon, but when you live out the back end of Woop Woop and a cold beer is a two-hour drive, and you don't have a telephone, well that's how it started.

Bluey flicked a fly from his eye and listened as Ol' Bill got around to telling the story, and a mighty good story it was too.

'So I said to Maylee, I said, we gotta get organised. I said to her we want to get the internet. It's the thing ya see. The internet.

Bill said it like … in-ter-net.

'We can do things with the in-ter-net.'

'What like?' Bluey asked. He picked at the bark on the old stump next to his verandah and shooed a fly. Ralph, his whip smart kelpie, snapped at the fly, he rarely missed.

'Well, now ya talkin'. Ya can order anything ya like.'

'Like what?'

'Well…ya know, anything.'

'Like what?' Bluey pushed his hat back revealing a white bald head that had never seen the light of day. It looked like he only washed to the line and no further.

'Well, anything.' Bill nodded and smiled revealing a mouth with tombstone teeth, three in all. He had his good set of dentures, but they were a pain in the butt, as he liked to describe them. Maylee tried to make him wear them, but he said,

'If I'm drivin' all the way to Bluey's place, I don't need 'em. It's only Bluey anyways.'

He got as far as the black stump and popped the suckers in his top pocket, cursing his wife.

'What about teeth,' Bluey said and grinned.

'I guess.' The dig went so fast over Ol' Bill's head it nearly took his hat off.

'So anyways,' Bill resumed. 'We're gettin' it. The in-ter-net and Maylee said I was to invite youse all. Bill spread his hands wide over the homestead, although at the time the boys were fencing on the north paddock, the foreman was in the dunny and the owner was away buying cattle. 'Ya know, to see the in-ter-net. She's got to telephonin' everyone, but you don't have the tel-e-phone, so she said I should, ya know…well…ya know.' Bill scratched the back of his neck. Issuing invitations wasn't in his line of work, He was more of …'Who's shout?' kind of man.

'Bit of a do'.

'A do.'

'Yeah, a do.'

'Oh, and there was a telephone call, from your sister.'

'Me sister?'

'Yeah.' Bill fished about in his top pocket, put his teeth on the verandah rail and produced a piece of paper. 'May wrote it down.'

Bluey took the paper and looked at the words. The ink had run, *I won't give you two guesses how*, and tried to decipher the message.

'Moon… cracked…horrible?'

'What?'

'That's what it says, look for yourself.' Bluey handed the paper to Bill.

'I don't have me glasses. Anyways, May said it was urgent. Ya know, kinda ur-gen-t.'

'Well what the bloody hell is it?'

'May said ya mum's crook. In 'os-pi-tal.'

'In hospital.'

'Yeah. Something about her woman's bits, or somethin'.'

'Strewth.'

'Yeah.' Bill shuffled his feet. He wasn't one for discussing women's bits, mate or no mate.

'So, ya comin' to the do?'

'The do?'

'Yeah, only May needs to know. Caterin' and all that stuff. Sausage rolls and stuff.'

'Right. Then I guess I gotta go ta the big smoke.'

Bill nodded. 'I guess.' He looked at Ralph who was pissing on his truck wheel. 'Get out of it.' Ralph gave Bill a withering stare and trotted away.

'Ya know, with the in-ter-net ya could send her flowers. Women like flowers.' Bill thought he knew a thing or two about women.

'Flowers.' Bluey looked at the dust around the homestead. The only wet patch for a good 100 kilometres was Ralph's piss.

'So…the do?'

'Yeah, yeah. The do.'

Nev Peterson emerged from the dunny and hoiked up his strides. He was built like a brick shit house, so they said at the pub. As the foreman of Sawtooth Gully homestead he was in charge and knew how to handle the rouse-abouts. He walked up to Bluey, his leading hand, and they watched Bill's old truck drive away, the dust drifting up from the road for a good 4 kilometres until it was out of sight. He reckoned it would be dark before Bill got back to the pub.

'So what'd he want?' Nev waved a fly away.

'Got a phone call. Me mums crook.'

'Crook eh?'

'Yeah.' Bluey kicked the dust with his foot.

'She's crook then.'

'Yeah.' Bluey squinted into the sun bringing his dry gnarled hand up to his eyes.

Nev spat and Ralph looked at the wet patch with little interest.

'S'pose you gonna go an' see her.'

'S'pose so,' Bluey said.

The conversation finished and Nev headed to the sheds. He turned and said,

'You taking the ute?'

'Bloody oath I am.'

Nev's laugh could be heard for a good five minutes as Bluey turned to walked back to the bunk house. He looked at his ute and scratched his head.

'Nothin' wrong with the ol' girl,' he said to Ralph, and then he saw them. Ol' Bills choppers were still resting on the verandah rail.

'Bloody Nora.'

Ralph gave them a sniff. 'Git out of it.'

Bluey lay down on his bunk and stared at the fly spotted ceiling. He wasn't one for just uppin' sticks and goin' to the big smoke, just like that. These things needed to be thought over, chewed a bit. He put his hands behind his head and gave a tuneless whistle.

'Whaddayareckon Ralph?' Bluey asked his dog.

Ralph sat at the back door in indecision.

As a dog, he had distilled his life to about two choices. He knew the fridge held all that life had to offer, he also knew outside was where he wanted to be.

'The big smoke eh?'

Ralph turned in a circle and settled down on the mat. He snapped a fly. Never missed.

A cold beer was 2 hours away. The Big Smoke was a dry, dusty 10 hours on a good day.

To look at Bluey you'd think he was an overcooked leg of lamb. Years – decades in the sun had given his skin a hard time. His face was baked to a crisp, but his small blue eyes were enough to light up his face. He always had a look of wonderment mixed with innocence that had seen him in good stead every time he was headed for trouble.

'How could someone who looked so innocent, or gormless get in so much strife?' Nev often said.

Not that Bluey courted trouble, but he just happened to be standing by – backing the wrong horse, getting his Arthurs and Marthas mixed up and generally ending up holding the wrong end of the stick. (the Arthur and Martha yarn worth a good 6 schooners of beer and a long afternoon). Bluey had all his own teeth, always a good sign and had lost most of his hair by the age when looking for a sheila wasn't on his bucket list. He was suited to the landscape like a gum tree to a river bank. His only vice was picking his toenails and leaving the droppings about the place, much to the annoyance of Cricket who was eating nuts one night watching the tele and popped one of the morsels in his mouth by mistake. It was a story that brought a wry smile to Blue's face. Blue was that kinda bloke.

Now he packed his ute with his swag and dog biscuits, grabbed an old iron picket fence post and opened the bonnet. It was still early, but the resounding thump Blue gave the starter motor was enough to wake the dead. Nev shot out of the bunk house with his strides at half mast, a rifle cocked in his arm.

'What in the bloody blue blazers,' he reached the stock yard and saw Blue with the bar in his hand.

'Just goin' Nev.'

'In that,' Nev pointed. He was joined by Johnno and Cricket.

'He's startin' the ute.' Johnno nudged Cricket and they sat on the stockyard rail to watch.

Bluey had it down to a fine art.

He had to thump the solenoid for the starter motor, then put a brick on the throttle pedal and with an old thong hooked over the gear lever and attached to the cigarette lighter to keep in in first and a stick to operate the clutch he reached in and turned the key while pushing.

'Ya could give us a hand instead of sitting on the fence like a lot of galahs,' Blue shouted.

'Better than the tele.' Cricket, the youngest of the ringers, said.

'Buggers.' Bluey at 50ish wasn't getting any younger. He had a gut, aka beer muscle that could qualify him for the Olympics, his legs were stocky and past their prime and his feet were no end of trouble with a bunion and as Cricket said, more corns than the feed lot.

'Go on Blue. Give it a crack.' Johnno laughed.

'Git.' Bluey opened the door and began to push while turning the key. The engine kicked and stopped. The process was repeated several times to cheers and claps from the audience before it roared into life. Of course, the trick was to hop in before it took off in first. More than once Bluey had been seen running after the ute holding his strides up with one hand and grasping at the tail gate with the other.

'He's good mileage alright,' Johnno said as he wiped the tears of laughter from his eyes.

Blue lunged at the cab and pulled the brick from the accelerator pedal and whipped the thong from the gear lever. The ute began to idle.

'Nothin' to it.' He took a bow and the boys clapped. Next, he whistled up Ralph and the dog jumped through the window into the passenger seat and looked ahead. Blue tucked in his singlet and sat in the cab.

'Sprucin' yourself up eh Blue? For the big smoke and all them sheilas,' Cricket joked.

'Quit it,' Nev gave Cricket a fatherly clip over the ear. 'His mum's crook you know.'

'Sorry.' Cricket looked at his boots.

'Right, I'm off.' Blue waved to his mates and with a once around the yard he turned and headed east into the rising sun. The two hour drive was easy in the cool of the early morning. Blue and Ralph passed the time in silence, one on the lookout for roos the other on the lookout for roadkill. Ralph was quite partial to a roll in roadkill. Once, when Blue wasn't looking Ralph excelled himself and thereafter had to ride on the back tray of the ute for about a week before the stink faded. He had a keen nose for carrion.

They pulled into the Peninsular Bar and Grill car park next to three road trains and Bluey kept the engine running.

Ralph watched from the passenger seat as Bluey knocked on the pub's door.

'Bloody hell. What time do ya call this?' Bill stood at the door of the pub in his underpants and a singlet that might have been used as a rag to wipe the underside of a dunny seat.

'I'm goin' to the Big Smoke.'

'Oh.' Bill scratched, *inappropriately*.

'Yeah. But I'll be back for the do.'

'Right.' Ol' Bill picked something from his singlet, scrutinised it, decided it wasn't edible and flicked it on the ground. Ralph licked his lips.

'Goin' to me sisters.'

'Ok.' Bill hoiked his jocks up leaving little to the imagination, re-adjusted the tackle and held out his hand.

"Right.' It was one of those moments. Bluey saw the outstretched hand. He knew where the hand had been.

'Ok then.' He slapped Bill on the back and took the steps two at a time just as Maylee came to the door. She squinted into the rising sun and held her kimono wrap close to her chest.

'Is that you Blue?'

'Leave it woman.' Bill cautioned his wife. 'He's off to the Big Smoke.'

'Your mum?'

'Yeah.' Bluey said as he opened the door of the ute.

'You'll be back for the do?' Maylee called, 'because…'

'He'll be back.' Bill waved and shut the door on his wife. He knew a thing or two about women.

Ralph was the ideal companion on a long drive. He didn't talk too much, he was always awake and he could be occupied for hours just hanging out of the window letting his slobber dribble all over the door.

Blue slowed as a mob of kangaroos bounded across the plains. They were skittish and could change direction at a moment notice. Once, when they had been fencing out west, they hit a roo and Ralph tore out of the ute in hot pursuit only to end up with a deep scratch over his eye. He nearly lost his eye, but never his nerve.

The sun began to blaze in the sky, and the trip turned hot and the scenery monotonous. At three hours Bluey stopped for a stretch at Mackley's Crossing knowing the black top would start in another 20 clicks and the driving easier. He left the ute idling and watched Ralph jump out and go for a wander, then his gaze turned to the dust rising in the distance. It was a road train. Blue watched for a good 10 minutes before it came within spitting distance. It came to a halt at the crossing, the air brakes hissing and then the dust settled over the salt bushes, the ute and the big rig.

'Alright.' Bluey waved at the driver.

'Is that you Blue?'

'Mate.'

'Mate.' Blue stepped up to the cab.

'Bluey bloody Blue. Geez, your lookin' good.'

'Mate.' Bluey looked up. 'Gordy, Gordy Gordonson.'

'G'day.' A bulky arm with a thick tattoo extended from the cab and gave a wave.

'You goin' south?'

'Yeah, me mums crook.'

'Crook eh?'

'Yeah. Crook.'

'Geez.'

'Yeah.' The exchange wasn't worthy of a hallmark card, but it was full of the caring, sharing stuff in a blokey type of blokey way.

'South.'

'Yeah.' Blue said.

'Crook?'

'Yeah.' Blue responded.

The chit chat over Gordy waved, 'well, see ya Blue.'

'See ya Gordy.' The window was wound up and the Kenworth's engine began the laborious job of pulling three trailers for the next 500 klicks to the roadhouse and the turnoff north.

Blue watched the truck disappear and turned around to do a double take.

A man was standing on the side of the road, in white pantaloons and flowing top, his cardboard suitcase in hand and wearing a hat strung with corks.

'Hello.'

'G'day.' Bluey stuck his hands in his pocket and frowned.

'I am hoping you can take me to the city.'

'The city?'

'Yes. Please. If it is not too much trouble.' The stranger smiled and shooed a fly.

Bluey pushed his hat back on his head and scratched what was left of his red hair.

'Mate.'

The stranger smiled. 'Mate.'

'I am Adb al Hakim.'

'Bluey, and this 'ere is Ralph.' Ralph circled the man and gave him a sniff.

Ralph sat in the middle seat and fixed his one good eye on the interloper.

'Dog,' the stranger pointed.

'Ralph.' Ralph blinked and stared some more.

'Look Abdul. Ralph stays.'

'I am Adb al Hakim.'

'Abdul.'

'Adb al Hakim.'

Ralph barked and Hakim jumped, moving a little closer to the door hugging his suitcase to his chest.

'He is looking at me.'

Blue put the ute in gear and they gathered speed on the hard dirt road, leaving a trail of dust.

They had travelled for 40 minutes when Hakim coughed politely,

'Are we going to the city, I have a hairdressing appointment.' It was said in his best English.

'Strewth. Bit of a hike for a shearin' shed.'

'Pardon?' Hakim opened his suitcase and brought out his dictionary. He snapped the latch shut before Ralph could sniff the contents.

'Strewth?' He thumbed through the pages.

'I do not understand?' Hakim said.

'Mate?'

The next 20 minutes were in silence. Blue stole a glance at his passenger every 5 kilometres or so, looking for some hint as to his story.

'What's your story mate?'

'Story?' Hakim flicked though his dictionary.

'Ah, story.' He found the definition in his Farsi/English book. It was just a pity the book was about 80 or more years out of date. Useful phrases like, I would like to make a trunk call and, my polo pony needs a new shoe might have worked when the British Empire was in full swing, but knowing to ask where to procure a donkey and slave for your expedition just didn't cut it.

'I am Hakim.'

'Got that.' Blue hung his elbow out the window and steered the ute with his beer gut while he fished about in the glove compartment for a forgotten lollie. His fingers found Bill's teeth.

'Bloody Nora.' He pulled out the dentures and Ralph perked up. 'Bloody Bill.' The teeth were re-interred in the black hole that was the glove compartment. Ralph whimpered and looked longingly at the shut compartment. Hakim watched, wide eyed. Blue went fossicking once more and found a boiled sweet. He carefully peeled the cellophane and popped the morsel in his mouth.

'Sorry, only got the one.' Blue shrugged and took the wheel from his co-driver, aka beer muscle.

'That is ok Joe.' Hakim opened his suitcase and produced a bag of mints. 'I have.' Ralph licked his lips in anticipation.

If you have ever given a dog a chewy mint you will know how much slobber a dog can produce. Ralph took the mint as a peace offering and then proceeded to slobber. He dropped it on the seat and picked it up several times, but it always had the same effect. Hakim tried to move a little closer to the door as Ralph chewed, then…finally swallowed. He settled down and stared at the road ahead.

'Ralph.' Hakim said.

'Yeah, that's Ralph.'

'I am Hakim.'

'Abdul.'

After another 10 kilometres Blue tried again.

'So Abdul, where ya from?'

'I am from Iran.'

'I-ran?'

Hakim nodded and smiled, 'Pleased to meet you.'

'Mate.'

'Are we going to the city?'

'The Big Smoke.'

'This is my first time in New Zealand.'

'Nah, mate. This is Straya.'

'Straya.' Hakim opened his dictionary/phrase book. He stared in concentration at the pages and then shut the book and smiled.

'I am Hakim.'

'Abdul.'

At 50 kilometres Blue stopped the ute keeping it idling.

'Need a slash,' he said to his passenger.

'Slash?'

'Yeah, ya know. Bleed the lizard,' Blue explained.

'Jolly good.' Hakim hopped out of the car and brushed down his flowing trousers. He began to follow Blue into the scrub.

'What's your game?'

'Game?' Hakim looked it up.

'Cricket?'

'Nah, you stay there.' Blue whistled Ralph and told the two of them to,

'Stay.'

'So,' Bluey began when he returned, 'you one of them gays or somethin'.'

'Pardon?'

'Ya know, gay.'

Hakim thumbed through his dictionary. The definition said,

Gay: to be happy go lucky, carefree...in Farsi of course.

'Yes. I am gay. All the time gay.'

Blue took a good look at his companion. 'Thought so. The dress was a dead giveaway.' Hakim smiled and nodded.

'I am Hakim.'

'Abdul.'

With the three settled in the cab, Hakim offered his mints. Ralph was up for the challenge. He rarely refused food.

'Ta.' Blue popped the lollie in his mouth and the 'freshness' of the mint took him by surprise. He coughed and spat and stalled the engine. The ute rolled to a standstill and the flies took the opportunity to invade the cab.

'What they made of, dynamite?'

'They are very fresh.' Hakim chewed and smiled. Ralph was gushing all over the seat. 'It is a pleasant evening.'

'Bloody Nora.' Blue hit the steering wheel, swatted at the flies and slumped in his seat. Outside was hot. A stinker. The cab wasn't much better.

He looked over to Abdul. He was thin, but looked strong enough.

'You'll need to push.'

'Push.'

'Push.' Ralph hoiked his thumb to get out the back. He mimed the action of pushing the ol' girl.

'Ah.' Hakim jammed his hat on his head and rolled up his sleeves, then hopped out of the ute. He stood at the back and placed his hands on the tray.

'I am beginning,' he shouted.

'Push,' Blue shouted. Hakim put his back into the task.

'Bloody push.'

'PUSH,' Hakim shouted. The dirt road was a mixture of pebbles specifically designed to hurt your feet and dry sand that did nothing more than make you slip and get in your socks. Hakim put his shoulder into it.

Blue tried. The car stalled and Hakim fell in the dirt. He picked himself up and tried again. The ute bucked and spluttered and died.

'Bloody Nora.'

'Bloody Nora,' Hakim echoed. He was a quick learner. Bluey tried the star picket on the solenoid. He thumped. Hakim pushed. The ute refused.

'Bugger.'

'Bugger.'

'You said it mate.' Blue sat in the cab and looked at the straight dirt road ahead. Ralph snapped at a fly.

The three sat for some time looking at the road.

'Are we going to the city?'

'Right, let's do it.'

Hakim pushed the ute, and Bluey employed his brick and stick, giving it his all. The ute spluttered and died.

'Shit.'

'Shit.'

The mints were eaten with resignation. All they could do was wait for a passing car.

After an hour, Blue said,

'So how come Straya.'

'Pardon.'

'What cha doin' here?'

'Ah.'

Blue grabbed the dictionary and squinted at the small lettering. He pointed to each word to convey the meaning.

'Ah.' Hakim nodded.

It took about three hours, but slowly the story emerged, and a good story it was too.

'I am coming to make good work. I am driving the taxi.'

'Bloody hell.'

Ralph barked and the two men looked at the road. There, in the far distance was a bloke walking.

'Bloody Nora.'

'Bloody Nora.'

Tommo walked up to the ute, bent down to the driver's window and waved a fly away.

'Knew it was you. I said to Charlie, that's Bluey.'

'G'day Tommo.'

The ute was now surrounded by 5 aboriginals. Tommo, Charlie, Roger, Chook and Jacko.

Hakim hugged his suitcase and wound the window up as the fellas gawked at him.

'What cha got there Blue?' Charlie said as he peered in the driver's window.

'He's from I-ran,' Blue said.

'I-ran.' Chook said. 'Where the bloody hell is I-ran?'

'It's them Arabie countries.' Jacko came up to the ute passenger window and knocked on it.

Hakim hugged his suitcase a bit tighter and began to pray.

'What cha doing Blue?'

'Goin' south. Me mum's crook.'

'Crook eh?'

'Yeah.'

'I think he's scared of us.' Chook made a face at Hakim.

'I am in need of,' Hakim began when Jacko hit the window with his hand.

'He can speak.'

'Sorta.' Blue answered.

'We're gonna camp here tonight.' Jacko indicated a patch of scrub off the road.

'Wanna give us a push. Me ol' girl's gone lame.' Blue thumped the steering wheel.

'Bloody Nora,' Hakim said.

The lads moved to the back of the ute.

'Get out.' Blue thumbed the message and Hakim shook his head, his eyes bouncing around on stalks.

'Git.'

Hakim opened the door and looked at the boys. He smiled, 'I am Adb al Hakim.'

'Abdul,' Blue shouted to the lads. Chook pointed. 'He's got a dress on.'

'He's a poofter.' Blue said, 'and no two ways about it.'

'Oooo,' chook made a girly face.

'Just get on with it.' Roger chipped in.

'Right.' Blue put the ute in gear, his foot on the clutch at the ready.

They pushed.

The ute spluttered and died.

They pushed.

The ute juddered to a stop and the boys fell about laughing as Hakim landed face down in the dirt. He hopped up and brushed himself down and took his position once again.

'He's game any-roads.' Charlie spat on his hands and stood next to Hakim. The others took their place and they pushed the ute then Bluey tried the jump start again.

'Bugger.'

'Bugger.' Hakim said.

'Too right brudda.' Roger slapped Hakim on the back.

'Ya want us to push ya all the way Blue, cause it ain't workin'.' Charlie sat down in the shade of a bush at the side of the road.

'She's stuffed I reckon.'

'Stuffed,' Hakim said.

Ralph followed the boys to the clearing and revelled in the attention. He went from one to the other for a back scratch, a rub on the ear and a game of chase the stick.

Blue fetched his swag and threw it on the ground. He looked at Hakim.

'Ya not sharin'. Blue shooed Ralph from his swag.

'We are not going to the city?'

'Not even if ya beg.' Blue went to get Ralph's biscuits from the ute.

Tommo, sidled up the Hakim.

'We used to eat you whities.' He licked his lips and gave a leering stare at Hakim. It was enough to make the poor fellow jump out of his skin. He raced to the ute and bumped into Blue coming the other way.

'Jeez mate. The whole bloody Straya and ya pick me. Here take this.' Blue handed the dog biscuits to Hakim and returned to the ute.

He came back with his gun.

'Tucker.'

'Beauty.' Charlie started to gather wood for a fire.

'C'on Abdul. We gotta eat.' Blue said. Hakim set the biscuits down and jammed on his hat.

'Eat?'

'Wha?' Charlie frowned.

"Sall right. He's readin' the bloody book.' Blue said. 'Some sorta book for foreigner types.'

Blue whistled up Ralph and the unlikely threesome set off in the bush.

'Reckon we could see a turkey.' Blue stopped and looked at a small mound under a bush. Hakim swatted at the flies.

'Keep still will ya.' Blue grabbed his hand and put it by the man's side. He indicated they should watch the mound.

A bird appeared. It began to scratch. Blue cocked his gun and let off one shot. The bird fluttered in the air and then fell.

'Got cha.'

'Got cha.'

They walked back to the camp with the bird and were joined by Charlie with a lizard and Tommo had another bird. All the food was thrown on the fire and then Chook produced a flagon.

'I knew you'd have some steam.' Blue slapped the young lad on the back.

'Me mum said I couldn't come home 'til I was sober. Gotta drink the lot I reckon.' Chook cackled with laughter. He looked over to the small humpy behind a bush.

'We got a home brew goin'.'

'Crikey.' Blue said.

'The good shit.' Chook said with a grin. It was more rubbing alcohol than drinking alcohol.

He took a good long swig and passed the drink around.

'Nah. Me mum will kill me.' Tommo passed the flagon to Charlie.

'Nup. I promised me missus.' He passed it to Jacko.

'You gotta be kiddin' me. I'm playin' footy tomorra.'

Jacko took the flagon and looked at the contents. He handed it to Roger.

'Nope. I gotta a missus with a mean left hook.' He passed it to Blue.

'I'm drivin'.'

'In the ute?' Chook asked and began to laugh. 'That heap of shit.'

'And I don't see your Toyota anywhere,' Bluey said.

'He's right Chook.' Jacko grinned.

Bluey passed the flagon to Hakim. They all looked at the stranger.

'Thank you.' He sniffed the contents. Everyone watched.

'Drink.' Chook offered.

Hakim smiled. The contents went in and came out at the same velocity. Hakim spat and the alcohol hit the fire with a ferocity that made the flames jump several feet in the air. The group scattered in all directions.

'Jeezus.' Chook snatched back the bottle and put the lid on.

'He's bloody dangerous.'

'For a poof.'

'Poof.' Hakim echoed and smiled.

As the sun went down the insects came out for take away.

Hakim began to swat, slap and itch. The others didn't seem to be bothered by the blood suckers.

'You gotta sit in the smoke,' Blue indicated Hakim should move closer to the fire.

'Tucker?' Johnno chipped in.

Roger hooked the meat from the fire and put everything on some paper plates he found in the humpy.

'We goin' fancy eh?' Chook took his plate. Blue pulled at the turkey and handed some to his new friend.

'Eat,' he mimed.

Hakim looked at the burnt offering on his soggy paper plate.'

'It's a BBQ.' Johnno said.

'Mate,' Bluey said.

'Mate,' Hakim replied and picked some meat off the bone. They all watched as he tried lizard. He chewed and smiled, nodding profusely.

'I think he likes it,' Chook said.

The party relaxed and then Roger said,

'So Blue, what's his story?'

Blue wiped his greasy fingers on his singlet and sat back. He was in an expansive mood.

'Well,' he began. His audience relaxed on the ground. Ralph found the bones, had a meal and went to sleep as close to the fire as he could get without cooking.

'It all started with a phone call.' Blue began at the beginning. 'And then Gordy Gordonson just drove off and he was standin' there.'

The boys listened as Blue continued.

'He's from I-ran. He's a taxi driver.'

Hakim nodded. 'Taxi.'

'Apparently,' Blue caught the attention of the crowd, 'he was on one of them people smuggler thingos and they said for a price they would drop him off in bloody New Zealand.'

'New Zealand?' Johnno said.

'Yeah. He thinks he's in New bloody Zealand.'

Hakim nodded, 'New Zealand.' This sent the lads into fits of laughter. Every time Hakim said New Zealand they found it hard to stop.

'Quit it.' Blue wiped the tears from his eyes.

'I told him we're in Straya.'

'Country,' Tommo said and picked up a handful of dirt and threw it on the fire.

'He said he wants to, you know, stay and stuff.'

'There's no sheep here.' Charlie said and the boys smirked.

'So, you know, where did he get off the, you know, boat?' Johnno asked.

'Dunno. Up the gulf I guess.' Blue shrugged.

Hakim smiled,' I am Hakim.'

'Abdul.'

'So why'd he leave, you know, I-ran.'

'Dunno?'

'Why'd ya leave Abdul?' Charlie asked. Hakim brought out his dictionary and by the light of the fire he added to the story.

'I am leaving my country.'

'Yeah, we got that.' Blue said.

'I am leaving or I will be dead.'

'He says he was told to leave or…' Charlie drew his finger across his throat.

'Bloody Nora,' Bluey said.

'Geez,' Chook's eyes widened. 'Is that 'cause he's a poof.'

'Could be.' Charlie looked at Abdul and then in a show of comradery patted him on the back. Their idyllic life of the bush, the fresh air, family was a world away from events that hit the papers.

'What about his mum? Ask him.' Chook said.

'Family,' Charlie thumbed through the dictionary.

Hakim's easy smile disappeared.

'I have brother, sister, mother, father. I am leaving them.'

'He bloody had to leave 'em all.' Charlie frowned.

'Poor bugger.' The men sat in silence and digested the information. Family was everything.

'It's the shits.'

25

'Too right. The shits.' Blue said.
'Shits.'

Chook staggered to his feet and disappeared into the humpy. He came back with a small stereo system. He pressed play and Zorba the Greek began. The boys took the music and made it their own. They pulled Hakim and Blue to their feet and then began to dance. It might not have won a prize on 'who's got talent', but the mood shifted and as the music blared out 500 miles from the nearest street light, Hakim found new friends amid the kicked dust, the music and the fire.

'Brudda,' Charlie slapped Hakim on the back.
'Brudda.'

Waking up in the desert in the morning isn't like waking up in a hotel. Bluey opened his eyes and looked at the sky. He stretched and then felt a hand around his copious girth.

There is nothing like a hand around your copious girth to give you a start. Blue shot out of his swag, coughed loudly, hurrumphed a few times, spat and checked his manhood.

Hakim was equally startled and jumped to attention, adjusting his attire and stretching outrageously, doing a few push ups and breathing deeply, like he did a daily dozen with one arm behind his back every morning.

'You awake then,' Blue coughed.

'Sobh bekheir,' (*good morning,*) Hakim said bursting into star jumps.

'Right then.' Blue looked to the East. The boys were strewn around the fire.

'Only got a dingo's breakfast.' Blue said. 'You know, a piss and a look around.'

'Ah.' Hakim nodded.

'Stay.' Bluey said and held up his hand. Hakim smiled and sat down as Blue grabbed some dunny paper and went for *breakfast,* followed by Ralph.

'Off ya go then,' Blue came back pulling up his shorts and a smile on his face. 'Nothin' like a good dump to get things back on track. It didn't happen often, but when it did, it was a miracle.

'Dump.'

'Ya know, choke a darkie.'

Hakim looked around the camp fire. There was one soul missing.

'Nothin' like it.' Bluey tucked his singlet in and farted.

Hakim put his hands to his throat and took a step back.

'Ya goin' or not?' Blue asked.

'Not.'

'Suit ya self.'

Charlie appeared from the hut with a tin and beckoned Hakim over for a look.

'They're a bit stale, but they'll do eh?' He opened the tin and handed a biscuit to Hakim.

'Thank you very much.'

'Not a problem Brudda.' Charlie took three and handed the tin to Blue.

'Where'd you get these, the Ark?' Blue took a few and gave one to Ralph.

'Nah. Dunno. Found 'em.' Charlie chewed.

'Is good.' Hakim said.

'So ya speak English then, Abdul?' Blue asked.

'I am speaking.' Hakim nodded.

'Yeah, got that.'

'I am learning New bloody Zealand.'

'It's Straya mate. Ya bloody in Oz-stray-ya.'

'Bloody Oz-stray-ya.'

'Yep.'

Tommo rolled over, 'Ya reckon we could draw a map maybe.'

'Got a lightbulb while ya at it, Einstein.' Roger said.

Tommo sat up and picked up a stick.

'Look 'ere.' He beckoned Hakim over to a patch of dirt.

'We're here.' Tommo drew a map of Australia and pointed to the middle.

'Here,' Hakim pointed.

'Yeah, an' New Zealand is here.' Chook woke up and took the stick and pointed somewhere over to the east. 'It's bloody cold in New Zealand.'

'Cold?'

'Brrrrr. Fuckin' freeze ya tits off.' Chook said by way of explanation.

Jacko yawned and took up the lesson. 'We're here,' he drew a circle and pointed to Australia.

'This is the equator.'

'Ah.' Hakim took the stick and drew the middle east.

'Now ya gettin' it.' Roger stretched and propped himself on his elbow, looking like he liked a lie-in on a Sunday morning.

'This is Iran.' Hakim pointed.

'I guess.' Charlie shrugged.

'And this is my home.'

'Home.' Jacko repeated. 'This,' Jacko picked up some dirt, 'this is our home.'

Hakim took the stick and drew a line.

'I start here. I go here.' He pointed to India. 'Then here,' he drew a line from India to Australia. 'On a boat.'

'Never.' Jacko frowned and shook his head.

'Is true. I come to New Zealand.'

'It's a long bloody walk to New bloody Zealand,' Blue said.

'Well can't ya drive him there Blue?' Roger quipped.

This last quip from Roger started them laughing.

'Now don't ya go slinging off. I don't see youz lot with four wheels any time soon.'

The biscuits were eaten, the fire kicked out and the flagons stored for another day when Blue hummed and hawed.

'Er…'

'Ya fussin' like a chook Blue, what's up.' Roger said.

'I was hopin' to get goin'. Ya know, to the big smoke.' Blue walked over to his ute and gave it an affectionate kick.

'So?' Chook asked.

'Well, I, um, I …'

'He wants us to bloody push it for him.' Charlie hitched up his trousers.

'Fair suck of the sav. I got a footy match this arvo. Savin' me strength.' Jacko said and began to walk down the road.

'I will push.' Hakim rolled up his sleeves.

'That's the way.' Blue slapped him on the back.

'Orright.' Jacko fell into line.

'Jeez,' Tommo and Roger joined the ranks.

'Bugger,' Chook and Charlie gathered their strength at the sides.

'Right, now I'm gunna give it a big kick when she's at full speed.'

'Git on with it.'

'PUSH,' Hakim shouted and then all obeyed.

Blue offered up a prayer to Murphy of Murphy's law and as the ute gathered pace he gave it one last try. It jerked, it spluttered and then it roared into life, taking off in a cloud of dust and leaving the lads behind.

'Reckon he'll be back?' Roger asked.

'Yeah,' Chook answered, 'he wouldn't leave Ralph.'

The dog sat in the shade of the men and snapped at the flies.

Bluey thumped the steering wheel and gave thanks heaven. He pulled up and did a U-turn and came back like a triumphant hero, although he hadn't actually done any of the hard yards.

'Beauty mate. 'op in.'

The lads piled in the back with Ralph and hoiked up Hakim then Charlie thumped on the roof, Blue put the ol' girl in gear and they headed for the township of Mungdeegi, population 56, at present 50 as 6 were in the ute.

'I am having a jolly good time.' Hakim said as the lads ate dust and bounced their way home.

'A jolly good time,' Charlie copied in his best English.

Mungdeegi consisted of about a dozen fibro houses, an oval for Australian rules footy, and a club house that doubled as the store. The ute threw up a dust cloud and came to a halt at the oval with the engine running.

'Thanks Bluey.'

'Nothin' to it.'

The lads jumped down and watched as Hakim pulled up his clothing and jumped to the ground.

'Ya reckon he's a poof?' Jacko frowned.

'Blue said.' Chook answered.

'Ya reckon he can play footy?' Jacko said looking at Hakim's athleticism.

'Ask him?'

'Hey Abdul, you play footy?'

'This is footy?'

'Footy, ya know,' Jacko mimed kicking a ball.

'Footy.' Hakim copied the footwork.

'Yeah, that's it.' Jacko nodded.

'I am.' Hakim nodded and smiled.

Jacko leaned in the cab, 'Hey Blue, Hakim wants to 'ave a go. We need a good runner.'

'What about me Mum?'

'It's only a couple hours and Winston can take a look at this piece of shit for ya. He can fix it proper.'

'Shit? This is premium engineering.' Blue said.

'Whatever ya say Blue.' Jacko laughed.

'A'right.' Blue drove the ute to the shade of a gum tree and turned it off. He offered up another prayer, not to Murphy, but Winston, the bush mechanic.

Shade is at a premium in the bush. Bluey and Ralph wilted in the shade of the lone gum tree as the shadows shortened to midday.

Hakim, on the other hand, was treated like royalty.

Charlie's aunty Lu took Hakim under her copious wing and ferreted him away to her house. It wasn't 20 minutes and the news had travelled around the compound that there was fresh meat, aka Hakim in town.

The women flocked around Hakim. He was new, different and quite handsome.

Aunty Mary brought out the raspberry cordial.

'Spiked with who knows what,' Nellie said.

Hakim, ever the gracious guest took the drink and sniffed.

'It's good eh?'

'Good.'

'Yeah.' Mary took a swig and smacked her lips. Hakim smiled and took a sip. He nodded as the drink slid down.

'Beauty Mate,' Hakim said.

'I taught 'im that.' Aunty Mary laid claim to Hakim's education and refilled his glass.

'Where ya from fella?'

Hakim licked his lips and smiled. He nodded, 'I am from Iran.' He held out his glass for another drink. Meeting Aunty Mary was thirsty work.

'He came in with Bluey.'

'Blue eh?'

'Yeah.'

'I-ran eh. Where the hell is I-ran.'

'Mum, it's one of them Arabie countries.' Dora, aside from being a footy umpire was top of her class at school.

'Da ya 'ave Smiths chips in I-ran?'

'Mum,' Dora rolled her eyes.

'Well, I dunno do I.' Mary pulled out a family pack of chips.

'They have camels,' Nellie offered.

'Cam-el,' she said to Hakim.

'Cam-el,' he echoed and smiled.

'I taught 'im that,' Nellie said and nudged Mary in the ribs.

'Handsome ain't 'e.'

'Mum,' Dora smiled at Hakim and twiddled her hair. At 16 years old Dora was of the opinion that anyone who wasn't from Mungdeegi was drop dead gorgeous, aside from Bluey of course, and a few ringers who often passed through, and the postman who had false teeth and bad breath, and relations – of which there was about 55. To pin it down, anyone under the age of 26 and didn't come from Mungdeegi. Hakim fitted the bill.

The smile fest was broken by Mary,

'Hang on, here comes the mob.'

Flo, Bet, Winnie, Wanda, Ali, Kath, Sue and about a dozen kids crammed into Mary's place and it was turning into a party.

'He's from bloody I-ran.'

The news was greeted with a cheer. Dora sidled up to Hakim and went all goggle eyed and plied him with cordial.

'Thank you very much. I am very thirsty.'

'He speaks real good lingo eh?'

'Mum.' Dora sat a little closer.

'Nice teeth.' Flo said peering at Hakim.

'He's not hitched, is he?'

'Nah. Don't reckon. I reckon he's one of them oil sheiks.' Bet said as she helped herself to a drink.

'Ya reckon?' Flo popped the lid on a tin of biscuits.

'Yeah, I reckon.' Winnie said helping herself to a biscuit. That was enough to make it a fact. Now the women just needed to get him married off, for mothers are the same the world over, and aunties too, for that matter.

'Mum,' Dora blushed. 'I gotta go. I'm the ump for the match.' She looked at Hakim, 'c'mon you,' she grabbed Hakim's arm and led him out of danger – although that could and would be debated for a few months in the future as a footy match in 40 degree heat on dirt that is rock hard and an opposing team that look like they train once a week and are out to win at any cost could be considered danger with a capital D; although Hakim didn't even know what the word meant and he'd left his dictionary in the ute. But for all intents and purposes he was going from the frying pan into the fire.

When you live in the bush getting 18 players together can be quite an ask. Jacko had been trying to get a mob together for the last two weeks. He was about 4 men short, 3 now Hakim had decided to take to the field. His sister volunteered as umpire and his aunty was the goalpost ump. He had bribed his uncle Billy to keep score, but as with all things in Mungdeegi anything could go wrong when you needed to rely on other people.

The opposing side rocked up in a mini-van. Bluey read the logo.

The Umbabalabgungadilliamumba and District Volunteer Regional Authority & Aboriginal Youth amalgamated local Government community funded institution Bus. The name took up the whole side of the 14-seater and ended around the back.

Blue and Ralph watched the team pile out of the bus. There were a few strapping lads, one that would rival a refrigerator for size and a gaggle of women. They all had shirts with UDVRA&AYALGCFI emblazoned on the front.

'Shit.' Jacko rubbed his chin as he looked at the team. His mob only had last year's NADOC shirts donated by the Southern Districts Footy association.

'Hey,' Dora shouted to her brother. She pulled Hakim along.

'He's playin'. Jacko pointed.

'Him?'

'Yeah. He's dead keen.'

'Deadly.' Dora's estimation of Hakim went up a notch. Handsome, young, an oil Sheik and plays footy. Her score card was full.

Hakim hadn't changed, he'd hardly had time to eat a biscuit, and as the raspberry cordial hit his blood stream and the heat took a hold of the top of his head, he began to feel like a bit of lie down and some cooling mint tea might just do the trick.

'Jeez, what happened.' Jacko looked at Hakim who was staggering.

'Aunty Flo, Aunty Bet, Aunty Winnie and Mum.'

The crisis was passed to Dora as the rest of the team began to arrive.

'Ya got the ball?' Chook asked.

'You said you'd have it,' Jacko held his head in his hands and they saw three of the team weren't wearing their boots.

'Where's ya boots,'

'They hurt Jacko. We just can't use 'em.' The team gravitated to the shade of the lone tree and sat down.

'Howdy Blue.' They flaked out and waited for something to happen. Whether it would or not only time would tell. Without a ball, the odds were somewhere between 50 to 1.

'Now I need to get a bloody ball.' Jacko went looking while swearing, stomping, swearing some more and tearing his hair out.

It was something to watch as the sun beat down.

Dora led Hakim to the club house and sat him down on the cool concrete floor. He felt his body would be better served lying flat out. He flopped down and closed his eyes.

'Stay there.' Dora went to hunt out a whistle.

The team from Umbabalabgungadilliamumba (and yes I just cut and pasted it, so let's call them Umbabal) had retreated to the other side of the oval and put up a gazebo emblazoned with their specific logo and brought out some eskies. These fellas were the business.

'Will ya look at that.' Chook pointed to the flaunted luxuries.

'Bloody Nora.' Blue licked his lips. 'Want me to just nip over and take a deckie at their kit?'

'Ya reckon?'

'I'm goin'.' Bluey struggled to a standing position and adjusted his hat. 'Won't be long.' He hoiked up his stubbies and Ralph followed at a trot.

'I'm gonna see if they got a ball.' Chook made a move to the other side.

'I'm goin' ta see about...' Neil, Simmo and the rest of the team followed Chook's lead.

The guy who looked like a refrigerator stood in the middle of the gazebo and watched the parade.

'G'day mate. Bluey and this 'ere is Ralph.' Bluey held out his hand. Mr Westinghouse took the offered hand and shook the living daylights out of Bluey's arm.

'Nice to know eh. G'day.' Mr Westinghouse slapped Bluey on the back as Blue eyed the coldies in the eskies.

'Wanna stubbie?'

'Bloody oath. It's a stinker today eh?'

'Yeah.'

'Hey,' one of the ladies from the opposition squawked. 'I know 'im. It's Simmo.'

'Aunty Kathleen.' Simmo went all shy.

'How's ya mum?'

'Good.'

'An' ya no good for nuthin' father. Getting' a zebra suntan I bet.'

'Nah, he's outta the lock-up.' Simmo kicked the dirt with his toe as the assembled audience listened. Chances are they all knew the good for nuthin' or were related to him in some way or other.

'Have a coldie.' Aunty Kathleen handed drinks to the Mungdeegi team.

Thirty odd people plus Mr Westinghouse taking up the room of three in the shade of a 3 metre by 3 metre gazebo can get cosy. It was a given that one half knew or was related to the other half. Cousins come in a variety of sizes.

The teams were getting matey, talking over the big news, – the supply truck that was due any day and the humdrum of every-day life, like the politician who was dropping by to have his photo taken.

'Reckon we'll get some kit-kats this time?' Simmo asked his aunty.

'I reckon.'

'I like Mars bars.' Chook chimed into the conversation.

'Me too.' Mal nodded.

'Nah, ya can't go past a Snickers.'

'You kiddin' me.'

Mr Westinghouse waded into the debate on chocolate treats. 'I reckon the best of the lot is …' The teams waited with baited breath as the fridge presided.

'It's gotta be a Violet Crumble.'

This pronouncement brought howls of derision. Apparently, the lads decreed, only girls ate honeycomb coated in chocolate.

'Nah, I like snakes,' Bluey waded into the growing fight.

'Snakes? What the …' Simmo began to laugh.

'Well, I like 'em and so does Ralph.'

'Ralph eats roadkill Bluey.' That was enough to stop Blue's choice of confectionary.

The debate began to heat up as the sun reached its zenith when Jacko came back with a ball.

'I got a ball.' He held the misshapen ball aloft. No-one took a bit of notice as the conversation veered towards the merits of Smiths crisps or Lays thins.

'I said I got a ball.' Jacko shouted over the ruckus. 'We playin' or what?'

The Umbabal team fetched another esky and the home team sat down to enjoy themselves.

You had to feel sorry for Jacko. He's set his heart on having a good Aussie Rules Footy match. He's been the grand organiser of the whole shebang and now it was a fizzer.

Dora came over to let her brother know she couldn't find a whistle.

'Where's the fella?'

'Flat out like a lizard drinkin'.' Dora pointed to the club house verandah.

'Well that's it then.' Jacko threw the ball down in a temper and it bounced out onto the empty field, and there it stayed, forlorn, alone and unloved.

'Bugger y'sall.' Jacko stormed off.

Dora fetched Hakim and led him back to the gazebo, grabbing her brother on the way.

'This is my cousin, Thelma. And this is my cousin, Rodney.' She threaded her arm in Hakims and smiled. 'He's an oil Sheik.' Thelma and Rodney nodded and handed Hakim a beer.

'Drink.' Rodney mimed.

'Good?'

'Better than good.' Thelma flicked the lid off the stubbie with a practiced air.

They watched as Hakim sniffed the drink. He looked at the bottle and mouthed the English.

'XXXX,'

'Yeah, Fourex.' Rodney said.

The tent quietened down as all eyes gravitated to the stranger in their midst.

'I don't think they have beer where he comes from.' Rodney said.

'Beer.'

'Yeah, mate. Beer.' Bluey said. 'Drink.' He showed Hakim there was nothing to it and chugged his beer in one.

'Who is he?' Mr Westinghouse asked.

'He's visitin'.'

'Ya can't have a ring in.'

'He's one of us.'

'Yeah, and I came down in the last shower.' Mr Westinghouse replied.

'It'd be the first one ya had for 'bout a year then.' Simmo said, hanging onto the gazebo for support.

'Ya gunna need more than a shower when I get through with you, ya drongo.'

'Drongo.' Chook began to laugh.

'What you laughin' at, ya mother called ya a chook.'

'Henry.'

40

'Hen-ry.' Simmo retorted.

'Chook,' Aunty Kathleen began to laugh.

'Chook?' Hakim frowned.

'Ya know, a chook.' Simmo mimed a chicken pecking in the dirt and flapped his arms.

'Ya a pretty good dancer Simmo, why don't cha go in for one of them shows on the tele?' Chook chuckled.

'Nah, don't wanna show 'em up.' Simmo stopped flapping.

'Where's ya book?' Bluey mimed the dictionary.

'Ah,' Hakim nodded and mimed a chicken laying an egg. He flapped. He squatted. He pushed like he was giving birth to something as big as … well he grabbed the football and sat on it.

This had the crowd in stitches.

Dora wiped the tears from her eyes and took a deep breath, Simmo and chook had collapsed on the ground.

'I think I got a stitch.' Simmo rolled over and everytime he laid eyes on Hakim he was off again.

'Give it a rest will ya,' Bluey wiped the tears from his eyes.

Hakim stood up and looked at the ball.

'Is game?'

'I'm bloody game.' Jacko snatched the ball and held it tight. 'We gunna play or what?'

The assembled mob looked at the dry, dusty, crunchy footy field. It wasn't an inspiring sight. The goal posts were shimmering in the heat and even the birds had the sense to retreat to the shade. The quiet was broken by the wonderful sound of a stubby being opened. That delicious music which ended with a satisfactory plink as the cap hit the ground and joined its many mates.

Jacko looked beaten. His shoulders slumped, his dreams dashed with the opening of a beer.

A flock of galahs started to screech in the nearby paperbark eucalyptus tree. The retort by the kookaburras was too much like mockery for Jacko.

He threw down the ball and someone's cousin gave him a beer.

'Bugger it.' Jacko slammed the cooling drink down and someone gave the man a chair. Alcohol can resign a man to the inevitable quicker than a woman at the jewellers with an empty ring finger. He hurrumped a bit, but it fell on deaf ears.

'What's his story Bluey?' Simmo looked at Hakim.

'Yeah, Blue, what's his story?' Mr Westinghouse added.

'Blue was feeling in an expansive mood. He cleared his throat as if he was a finalist at toastmasters and ran his tongue over his teeth.

'He's from I-ran.'

'Where the hell is I-ran.'

'I can tell you that.' Chook elaborated noting the equator, the sea, the trip and ended with,

'And he thinks he's come to New Bloody Zealand.'

'Bloody New Zealand.' Simmo laughed.

'Yes, I am wanting New Bloody Zealand.' Hakim nodded vigorously.

'Nah, this is Oz-tray-l-ia.' Aunty Kathleen said with a measured tone.

'Oz-tray-li-a,' Hakim mimicked.

That's the way.'

'I told him that,' Blue said.

Then Bluey strung out the yarn starting with the phone call.

'Ya mum's crook eh?'

'Yeah, crook.'

And so it went for about an hour and two more eskies of beers, soft drinks – 'cause some of the team were only

16 years old, and around 4pm when the sun had lost a bit of its bite someone suggested a sausage sizzle.

'So,' Dora sidled up to Bluey,

'Yeah luv?'

'He's not an oil sheik then?'

'Abdul, nah. He's a taxi driver.'

Hakim nodded, 'taxi.'

'So, um, he's not kinda one of them oil sheiks then?'

'Nah.'

Dora took a long look at Hakim and revised her list.

A sausage sizzle is the poor man's bar-b-que. It usually consists of white sliced bread, onions, dead horse and the cheapest sausages you can find at the shops. The BBQ at the footy ground had all the necessary ingredients.

A 44 gallon drum that had been gutted sideways and fitted with a metal plate served as the cooking venue. The fire was lit, the sausages procured from Uncle Billy's place, 'cause Uncle Billy was nowhere to be seen and he horded sausages like he was waiting for the price to rise, and things were cracking along nicely.

'Hey Abdul,' Tommo passed a sausage wrapped in bread and smothered with dead horse.

'Thank you very much.' Hakim took the offering and finished it in three bites.

'Bloody Nora.' Blue looked at his companion. 'I reckon he hungry.'

'Hungry,' Hakim said. 'Good.'

'Bloody oath.' Blue gave him another sausage which Hakim demolished in record time.

'Ralph?' Hakim pointed to the dog who was looking expectant.

'Not too many, they give 'im the farts.'

'Farts?' Hakim looked puzzled.

'Ya know, fart.' Simmo mimed the word with all the attendant noises.

Dora gave the whole thing a bit of a show by miming a big stink.

'Ah.' Hakim nodded and screwed up his nose. 'My mother she fart.'

This set the crowd off again.

'He's killin' me.' Simmo laughed until he collapsed.

'Yeah, and I gotta drive to the big smoke and if Ralph … well it's not … well it's not nice.'

'Nice.'

'Not nice.' Bluey nodded.

The sun went down, the beer and soft drink had been drunk and the sausages that didn't get eaten were burnt offerings to the magpies. If you wanted someone to take a look at your motor vehicle, now was not the time. A gutful of booze might be conducive to setting the world to right, but anything as tricky as Blue's ute would take a clear head.

'Nah, she'll be right.' Winston slapped Blue on the back and they sauntered over to the ute. A gaggle of stragglers followed.

'C'mon Abdul,' Jacko pulled Hakim to his feet.

Ralph jumped through the window into the passenger seat and settled in for an evening's entertainment.

'So what's the problem.' Winston began.

'It's a bag of shit,' a voice said from the back.

This elicited a round of laughter.

'Look, she's just hard to get started. She's a beauty once she's goin' but a bugger to get started.'

'Sounds like my missus,' a bloke quipped. There was a ripple of giggles and a bottle of rum was passed around.

'We need a light.' Winston peered into the innards of the motor.

'How 'bout the van,' Mr Westinghouse suggested.

Now any normal person would have thought to drive the van to the ute. Sweet as a nut.

But get two footy teams worse the wear for drink together and … well the next thing they were all pushing the ute around the perimeter of the oval – in the dark. That no-one thought to steer and Ralph wasn't up to the task it was a given that the ute crashed into the fence and kept going.

Hakim raced ahead and jumped in with Ralph and the ute ground to a halt around about silly mid on if there had been anything resembling a cricket pitch on the oval that doubled as the Simpson desert.

'PUSH,' Hakim shouted.
They all pushed.

Once the vehicles were in place, which necessitated getting rid of the fence and using the wood to restart the BBQ, the man of the hour, Winston, *'Bush mechanic extraordinaire'* took centre stage. He peered into the workings. Everyone took a look at the problem.

'She's finished.'

'Shot.'

'Buggered.'

'I reckon youz'd be up shit creek without a paddle.'

There were more than a few experts in the mob.

'I reckon she's fucked.'

The crowd parted as the final pronouncement was the majority consensus.

'Nah, she'll be right.' Winston inserted his head into the engine, grabbed something important and came up with a wire.

'Anyone got a hair clip?'

The men looked at one another. If they had a hair clip no-one was going to own up to it.

'Pffft.'

Someone coughed and there was a lot of shuffling of feet, a few hurrumps and clearing of throats.

'I got bottle opener,' someone offered.

'I got a pocket knife.'

'How 'bout a key ring.'

The men emptied their pockets looking for a bit of wire.

'I have.' Hakim took his suitcase and opened it, swatting Ralph's curiosity. He came up with a paperclip.

'You little rippa.' Winston took the clip and dived back into the engine.

'I have,' Hakim beamed and puffed out his chest in a manly show. There is nothing like being the saviour of the day to boost your standing in the community.

'We need a Jack.' Winston reappeared from the depths.

'Jacko, they need ya.' someone yelled.

'Nah, a jack, ya know to lift the thing.'

'Oh.'

'Should be one in the cab eh?'

'Sorry,' Blue looked a little sheepish. I broke a leg on me bunk a while back and used it.

'Goin' at it hard were ya?' Chook surfaced from the rum bottle.

'Git.' Blue gave him a nudge.

'Was it Gloria Blue or one of ya other sheilas?'

'Leave it will ya.' Blue blushed. 'I'd rather flirt with a boiled horse.'

'Bet it was Gloria.' Chook laughed until Jacko whacked him on the back of the head, either to knock some sense into him or the remnants out.

'Quit it.'

'Orright.' Chook retreated to the back of the ute and lay down in the tray.

'Well, we need somethin'.' Winston said.

'How about him,' Simmo pointed to Mr Westinghouse.

The fridge looked at the job in hand.

'Orright.'

There was the flexing, the stretching, the pulling up of the shorts and then as if the Olympic committee was watching Mr Westinghouse put his back into it. You'd think that someone would have had the forethought or common sense to grab a stump, a log, something to prop the ute once it was off the ground. This afterthought was debated for weeks after the chiropractor, the physio and the chemist who dispensed the pills had done their best to get Mr Westinghouse's back into the pillar of strength it once was.

He let out a yell, grimaced and gave, what Bluey described as, a face like a dropped pie, lurched then dropped the ute. Winston, who hadn't quite got under the job sprang out of the way as Jacko described like a roo on heat and the onlookers all took a step back with a,

'Whooooooooooo.'

It was a sight for sore eyes. Mr Westinghouse, who later was found to be Bubba Johnson who is related to the Johnson mob up north, had managed to get his stubbies hooked on the daggy number plate and as he dropped his bundle, his stubbies came down with it.

Now, I'm not an expert, but when you see a lad the size of a fridge with his daks down and you find he is wearing Teenage mutant ninja turtle underwear it's a bit hard not to crack a smile.

The lads did more than smile. They fell about laughing as Bubba pulled a face, tried to retrieve his dignity and failed as his back let him know who's boss. He howled and fell in a heap.

While everyone was otherwise occupied, Hakim helped Bubba to crawl to the van and lie down. He then retrieved the stubbies, folded them neatly and handed them over.

'Thanks mate.'

'Mate.' Hakim smiled.

'Bloody mob of ingrates.'

'Bloody mob.' Hakim said and nodded.

'No bull, you're welcome over our way any bloody time. Bubba winced as he made himself comfortable.

'Alright mate.'

'Too right. Mate.' Bubba held out his hand and they shook on the invitation.

'That should do it.' Winston felt the job finished if he got out alive. 'Bloody close-run thing eh?'

'Yeah, me little brother would've had them jocks.'

'Give it a rest.' Simmo stifled a laugh.

'Mate.'

'Mate.' Chook took a deep breath.

They all looked at the ute.

'Give her a run,' Simmo said.

Bluey eased himself into the driver's seat, gave the thumbs up and turned the key.

The ute, that mighty workhorse of the Australian outback, that master of the open road roared into life.

'Bloody beautiful.' Bluey went as far as to hug Ralph. Caught up in the moment Ralph licked Bluey and wagged his tail.

'Is good.' Hakim said.

'Is bloody t'riffic.'

'T'riffic'

It was just the thing to give the party a new lease of life. The bonfire was stoked, someone brought music, a couple of bottles of steam were produced and the coke machine was raided.

Bubba missed it all.

As the fire died, the opposition packed up and began the long journey home, Mr Westinghouse flat out in the aisle.

'Is Bloody Beautiful,' Hakim said as he lay on the ground looking at the stars.

'You said it.'

It was a perfect end to a great day.

'Doesn't get any better than this.'

Ralph farted.

B luey woke up to Ralph licking his face.
'Git.' He shooed the dog away and propped himself on his elbow to survey his surroundings. There were a few dead bodies strewn around the place, but nothing to get excited about.

'What you want?' Blue looked at Ralph whose tongue was hanging out.

'Ok, Ok.' Blue climbed out of his swag, stood up and hung onto the ute for support. 'Gis a minute.' He took a few deep breaths and then focussed on the club house. 'C'mon.' With slow measured steps Blue walked to the clubhouse and a tap.

He turned on the water and Ralph lapped it up.

'Sausages get to ya did they?' Ralph kept drinking. Blue put his head under the tap and had a bit of a scrub up. It wasn't much in the way of hygiene practices, but under the circs it would do. He put his hat back on and squinted into the rising sun.

'Abdul,' Bluey looked into the distance. He couldn't find him amongst the bodies.

For a fleeting moment Blue thought about leaving Hakim. There was a school bus that went as far as the next community, which was near the roadhouse, which always had traffic.

Ralph farted.

'Nup.' Bluey looked at his dog. 'If he gave you sausages, then he needs to suffer like the rest of us.'

Bluey whistled up Ralph and went in search of Hakim.

Some people have the knack of landing on their feet. Hakim was one of the lucky ones. Mary said Angel mentioned that Helen had told Ruth that Martha saw Nellie with him. Blue found him alright, by a circuitous route.

Hakim had his feet under the kitchen table of Aunty Nellie and she was feeding him cornflakes and toast.

'Will ya look at that,' Blue came to the screen door and shook his head. 'More front than Mark Foys.'

'Ah, come in Blue.' Nellie pulled another slice of bread out and put it in the toaster.

'Good morning to you.'

'I taught 'im that.' Nellie looked at her protégé.

Three kids hopped up at the table and tucked into their cornflakes.

'Children. John, Martin, Susan.' Hakim pointed.

'We taught 'im that.'

'Right.' Blue was given a cup of tea.

'Can we take 'im to school?'

'What?' Bluey smiled.

'I am going to the big smoke.' Hakim smiled. 'With Bluey and Ralph.'

'True.' Susan nodded. 'I wanna go ta the big smoke.'

'You wanna go anywhere,' Martin nudged her.

'Eat.' Nellie gave them a clip on the ear. 'An' hurry up.'

'You gunna see ya mum Bluey?' Nellie asked.

'Yeah, she's crook.'

'I heard. Crook eh?'

'Yeah, crook.'

'Will ya be back this way?'

'Yeah. I guess.'

'Ya couldn't get me a couple of things eh?'

'S'pose.'

Nellie brought out a list. The kids tried to see if there was anything like a scooter, a set of books about horses or a tennis racquet on it.

'Git,' Bluey held the list aloft.

'Git on the bus.' Nellie shooed her brood out and quiet descended on the kitchen.

'More tea Hakim?'

'Thank you very much.'

'I taught him that.' Blue said.

Ralph sat at the screen door and farted.

'Give me respects to ya Mum Blue.'

'Will do.' Bluey and Hakim walked across the footy oval to the ute.

'We go to the big smoke now?' Hakim asked.

'Yeah.' Blue hitched up his shorts and whistled up Ralph. 'Git.' Ralph jumped into the passenger seat and hung out the window.

'Thank you very much.'

Bluey squirmed. 'Yeah, well it's just a ride see, nothin' more see.' Hakim nodded and smiled. He squeezed in and pushed Ralph to one side.

'You goin' now?' Simmo strolled up to the driver's window.

'Yeah.' Blue hung his elbow out. 'Thanks for … ya know … well ya know.'

'Thank you very much.' Hakim leaned over Ralph and held out his hand.

'Yeah.' Simmo shook his hand then shaded his eyes and stood back as Blue did a U turn in the oval and headed out through the broken fence.

'How far is the Big Smoke?' Hakim said as they left the outskirts of Mungdeegi.

'Far enough,' and then Ralph farted. Hakim hung out of the window trying to breathe.

'Got a mint?' Blue held his breath.

From Mungdeegi to the turnoff the road is dirt. From the turnoff to Three Mile Drain the highway is graded dirt. From Three Mile Drain to Arnold's roadhouse is black top.

Blue and Hakim hung out of the window all the way to the black top. By the time they hit the bitumen Ralphs digestive system had excelled itself.

Hakim looked at Ralph.

'Fart.'

'You said it.' Bluey began to laugh and by the time they stopped at Arnold's roadhouse they were covered in dust with rivulets of tears etched into their faces.

'Jeez.' Blue got out of the ute and stretched. 'Ralph,' he whistled up the dog and said 'Git.' Ralph git.

'Eat?' Hakim mimed he was hungry.

'Too right. C'mon. My shout.'

'EAT,' Hakim shouted.

Arnold's roadhouse was legendary. There was the legend that he never changed his chip oil. There was the legend that he never owned a pair of jocks and scratched, and the all-pervasive legend that the meat in his burgers was something other than prime beef. The rumour that he was a serial killer and all the backpackers he ever employed never managed to last more than a week, was just fanciful. Still it brought in the trade. Arnold was, the truckies said, as skinny as a Scobie duck. If he ate, he didn't eat his own food, which could give you a heart attack just looking at the menu.

He was the quintessential serial killer type if ever there was one. The blurred and faded tattoos on his neck and forearms were reminiscent of gaol and his red eyes, missing teeth and hair style completed the police profile. Arnold had a mullet. That throwback hairstyle that was short on top and ridiculously long at the back. That Arnold's back bit was as thin as the bacon rashers on his egg and bacon rolls only added to the picture. The hair was also greasy and black.

His wife, Jean made up for Arnold in that she looked like she ate everything on the menu – twice. No-one could quite describe Jean because no-one could get past the big mole on her forehead. There was many a debate, out of earshot (about 400 klicks away) about the efficacy of an operation to remove her third eye. What Arnold and Jean saw in each other only God had the answer.

What they did have was a thriving business in the middle of nowhere.

That his was the only '*restaurant*' (and I use italics reservedly) within 370 clicks of the turnoff was neither here nor there.

Bluey pushed open the screen door and surveyed the clientele. He nodded to the truck drivers who were taking up most of the seats. They all sat alone, one to a table and looked up when the door opened.

'Sit,' Blue pointed to a, once red, Formica topped table and Hakim took the hint.

'Bluey? Is that you Bluey?' Arnold said.

'Yeah.'

'Ya fadin' away.

'Yeah, right.' Blue smirked. Arnold's hard sell didn't wash with Blue.

'Didn't come down in the last shower ya know.'

'So whaddleitbe? Jean asked as she poked a curling sandwich in the display counter, hoping to bring it back to life. A truckie once joked the defib paddles were in his cab and got banned for life. Not a great impost, as it turned out he saved himself a heart attack well into his 60th year.

Blue looked at the fly spotted menu above the chip fryer. Once there had been a garland of plastic ivy adorning the blackboard, but over the years the ivy had collected grease and now dripped cobwebs, fluff and something that looked suspicious and you wouldn't talk about in polite company.

'Umm.' Blue squinted.

'Well, I ain't got all day ya know.' In fact, Arnold did have all day. He wasn't exactly run off his feet. He scratched something hidden from view, (thank God) and swatted a fly.

'Well?' Arnold sucked his teeth and picked something from a molar with his finger.

'Two, ummm. Two house burgers and chips.'

'Nuthin' else?' Jean asked leaning on the counter and picking some left over food from the straw dispenser.

'Umm.' Blue was one of those people that just can't decide. Put a plate of food in front of him no questions asked and he'll eat the lot. Give him two pair of shorts to choose from and he could be all day getting ready.

'Ummm.'

'What about a milkshake.'

'Yeah.'

'Flavour?'

'Ummmm.'

'Jeez. Siddown will ya.'

Hakim waved to Bluey.

'Yeah, got that.' Blue squeezed his belly between the table and chairs. Arnold had long ago nailed the buggers to the floor to stop them being thrown about when someone actually got excited at getting fresh bread or something similar.

The pair waited in silence for their meal. Hakim smiled. Bluey smiled back. Hakim smiled some more. Bluey frowned.

'Just a ride, nothin' more see.'
Hakim nodded.

Blue, is that you Bluey.'
'Gazza?'
'Yeah.'
'Bloody hell.' Blue looked at the truckie.
'Where ya been?'
'Around.'
'Jeez.'
'Yeah.'
The exchange could have done with a quick course at toastmasters, but you can't have everything. Unless you have the house special burger at Arnolds.

Arnold sauntered over to the table and deposited two leaning towers of Pisa's on the table.

'Leave ya to it eh.'
'Yeah. Jeez. Gazza.'
'Yeah. Blue.'
'Seeya.'
'Seeya.'
'We EAT.' Hakim shouted.
'No need to shout.' Blue picked up the chips that had slopped off his plate, blew on them and put them back.

Arnold stood back and waited for an accolade.

'He one of them foreigners.' Arnold nodded in Hakim's direction.

'Yeah.'
'Foreign eh.'

'Yeah.' Bluey said. 'He's me mate.'

'Righty o.' Arnold ran his fingers through his hair, sniffed and retreated to the kitchen to contemplate his culinary delights.

'G'n, get stuck in.'

'Mate.' Hakim picked up his knife and fork and calculated how to attack the monster.

'Like this Abdul.'

Blue took the burger with both hands and squished it tight then took a large bite. The beetroot, the egg and the lettuce slid out the back. Blue then turned the burger around and poked the escapees back and took another bite.

For the inexperienced it rarely happens that the insides of the burger stay on the inside. Hakim tried, but his beetroot ended on his white shirt front and his egg on his lap. By the time he'd finished he had two buns and nothing in the middle.

The chips were easier to handle, but Arnold's chips were the fat greasy variety and very quickly if you are not slow and methodical they can end up like a boiled egg in your chest. Bluey ate like a slow wind-up toy, Hakim went in too fast, too soon. He thumped his chest and swallowed.

'You need a drink?' Blue looked at Arnold, 'How about them milkshakes.'

'Keep ya shirt on.' Arnold said.

'Couldn't work in an iron lung.' Blue slung the insult around the room and the truckies snickered in agreement.

Hakim grabbed his milkshake like a dying man in the desert. He sucked and the paper straw collapsed.

Everyone knows that if you put the straw in the dollop of ice-cream it comes up empty. Everyone except Hakim. His dilemma increased as the chips turned to stone in his chest. He grabbed the metal milkshake container and drank deeply. Half the contents went over the sides as those suckers aren't meant for mouths. Everyone knows that. Everyone except Hakim.

Hakim's performance was watched with silent fascination by the truckies. When you've been driving for 9 hours and the scenery is still one salt bush about 4 hours ago, anything is a diversion. Hakim stood up and his burger bits fell to the floor.

'Ralph.' He looked at the mess and giggled.

'Yeah, although I wouldn't feed this tucker to a dog.' Bluey finished his burger and ploughed on with his chips. 'Gives me indigestion.'

'Sit.' Bluey stood up and pulled out his wallet. 'My shout ok.'

'Shout?' Hakim frowned.

'Yeah, I'm gunna pay, ok.'

'Ok. Thank you very much.'

Bluey came back with a variety of lollies. 'Ya in for a treat, these are still in date,' which was a rarity at Arnold's roadhouse.

'Bloody foreigners.' Arnold looked at the mess left behind. Now he had to actually mop the floor. He might even find the pattern on the lino …. Stranger things have happened at Arnold's roadhouse.

'Bloody hell,' Hakim looked like he'd gone 10 rounds with Gordon Ramsey the famous chef and come off second.

Hakim giggled and shrugged as Ralph licked his lips and sniffed at Hakim's leg.

'Got clean clobber?'

'Pardon?'

'Ya know, duds.'

'Duds?'

'Yeah.' Blue took a pinch at Hakim's shirt.

'Ah.' Hakim went in search of his suit case with Ralph in hot pursuit.

'I have duds.' Hakim held up a blue shirt.

'It'll do.' Blue sat back on the ute's tray and waited for Hakim to change.

'Right, let's get crackin'.'

'Crackin' mate.'

'Hit the road.'

'Hit the road.' Hakim smiled and all three companions piled into the ute. Ralph leaned over and sniffed the glove compartment. He whined and pawed the latch.

'Git out of it.' Blue pushed him away.

'Bit of a hike now 'till we get to Farnham Homestead, then it's plain sailin' all the way to the big smoke.'

'We are going to the big smoke.'

'Too right.'

Hakim patted Ralph, 'Jolly good.'

'Whateveryasay mate.' Bluey started the ute first time, 'sweet as a nut.'

Around the half way mark somewhere near Woop Woop, there is a hill. Not a big hill, but big enough to stick out like a pimple in the otherwise flat landscape. Why the roadbuilders didn't just go around it, is one of life's mysteries. There is nothing for miles in any direction, but they had to build the road up and over. Mind you, the view at the top is quite nice, but it just makes you push your hat back and shake your head at the whys and wherefores of those blokes down south sitting behind a desk eating Monte Carlo cream biscuits.

Plinthe Hill loomed in the distance. Once you see it on the horizon it is the only thing you keep your eye on, and it takes forever to get any closer.

'Is the big smoke?' Hakim pointed to Plinthe Hill.

'Nah. Plinthe Hill.' Bluey looked at the pimple and wondered about physics and the nature of something looking like it was just about 10 minutes with a tail wind away, when in reality, as the crow flies, it was at least 20 kilometres or more … depending on the mirage over the road.

Hakim tried out the word. 'Pliiiiiith.'

'Nah.'

'Piiiith.'

'Nah. Pliiiinnnnnnnnththththt.'

'Pliiiiiiinnnnnnnnththththt.'

'That's about it.'

'What is Pliiiiinnnnnnththththth?'

'That.' Bluey pointed to the pimple that was now about 100 kiliometres away by his reckoning. 'It's a bloody hill.'

'Bloody hill.'

'You said it mate.'

They looked at the horizon and wondered if they would ever get to the hill such is the nature of physics and the Australian bush.

At the bottom of the hill there is a convenient parking spot should the eager tourist wish to stop and view the hill in all its majesty. The pull-off also has a wonderfully uninformative information board about the wildlife of the area which are nocturnal (nothing to see here citizen move along), the flora which is sparse (and probably poisonous) and the naming of the hill after an explorer names Plinthe; who came from somewhere and did something stupid like trying to walk to Alice Springs with a stick of liquorice and a box of matches. The sign was also peppered with bullet holes, a given in any rural Australian setting.

Bluey stopped the ute and looked at the incline.

'The last time was a bugger.' He climbed out of the ute.

'Bugger.' Hakim put his hands on his hips and looked at the hill. Bluey copied the stance and knew what Hakim was thinking.

'Nah, you won't need to push.'

At the word push Hakim's eyes widened and he scanned the horizon for a bus, a train, anything.

'Nah mate, I wouldn't do that to ya.' Bluey shook his head and Hakim visibly relaxed.

'I am needing a dingo's breakfast.' Hakim looked for a tree or bush for modesty.

'Eh?'

'Dingo's breakfast please.'

'Oh,' Bluey got the idea. 'It's called a piss mate. You gonna bleed the lizard.

Yes, I'm bleed the lizard.' Hakim walked off into the flat, sparse, desolate landscape looking for privacy. There was scant privacy to be had. He looked back once or twice, then nature took its course.

There can be few things to stop your bladder in full flow. A snake will usually do it.

Hakim watched the reptile slither in his direction. He wanted to shout. He wanted to run, but he was paralysed.

'Bluey,' he whispered. 'Bluey.' The name came out sounding like a strangulated cat.

A King Brown, the naturalist say, is quite venomous. Apparently, they tell us, it is one of the longest venomous snakes in the world and the second longest in Australia. Helpfully they say that it is uncommon to die within four hours of a snake bite.

'Bluuuuuuuuueeeeeeeey.' Hakim tried to remain perfectly still while his guts were doing cartwheels. The snake was intent on right of way and began to barge on through when Ralph came on the scene.

'Ralph.' Hakim tried to shoo the dog away, but Ralph was having none of it. He began to bark which upset the snake no end and a King Brown in a stroppy mood is best left alone. Ralph, being the show-off he was, began to prance and dance around the snake and bark.

Bravado comes in all shapes and sizes. Ralph had it in spades. Hakim watched as the dog circled the snake snapping at it and generally getting it in a bad mood for the rest of the day. The dilemma in all this for Hakim was a case of –

1: do you run like hell while the dog takes the heat.

2: do you try to save the dog from its own stupidity.

3: do you battle the snake.

Hakim took the first option. He lifted up his trousers and ran like hell shouting for Bluey.

Bluey, might be a little overweight, slow on the uptake and prone to indecision, but when someone is waving their arms about, shouting, pointing and running like a copper is after them he is the man!

He grabbed his rifle and bullets and cocked the gun.

Hakim on seeing the gun, ducked for cover – not that a flat landscape offers much cover, but you know what I mean – and Bluey lumbered past him and headed for Ralph.

A single shot rang out.

Bluey picked up Hakim from the dirt and Ralph began to jump all over him barking and licking and wagging his tail.

'Git.' Bluey pulled Ralph off.

'Bloody big 'un.'

'Bloody big 'un.' Hakim said and shook Bluey's hand.

'That'd be a King Brown.'

'Yes. Bloody big 'un.' Hakim began to brush himself down.

'Ralph thinks he's bloody got nine lives. Always havin' a go. One day though,' Bluey scrubbed Ralph behind the ear, 'one day it won't be so easy, will it fella.' Ralph rolled over and waited for a tummy scrub with Bluey's shoe.

'I could die.' Hakim was still in the moment.

'Nah, they don't like poofs. Can smell 'em a mile off.'

'Poof?'

'Yeah. Ya know. Poofs. One of them gays.'

'I am gay. I am a poof.'

'Got that.' Blue slapped Hakim on the back.

'Saved ya bloody life mate.'

'Thank you very much.'

'No problem mate.'

Bluey stowed the rifle in the ute and opened a packet of jubes.

'Want one?'

'Thank you very much.' Hakim took one and popped it in his mouth. It immediately tried to pull his fillings out and got stuck on his gums. Ralph had around about the same issues. Watching a dog eat a jube without the aid of a dexterous tongue can be quite funny. Hakim began to giggle at Ralph's antics. Ralph pulled his lips back and tried to chew. The gummy sweet was stuck and he slobbered more than usual.

'Jeez.' Bluey took control and flicked the lollie from Ralph's mouth and onto the dirt. It didn't stop him for asking for another. Dogs might be smart, but after all, they have a small brain.

'Right. Let's get crackin'.' Blue climbed into the ute and started her up.

'If ya like prayin' now's the time.'

Just to put you in the picture. The last time Bluey took the ute up Plinthe hill the ute went from 4th to 3rd to 2nd and then 1st but the diff threw in the towel when he couldn't go any faster than the roadkill. That workhorse of the Australian outback went backwards down the road and ended up at the parking spot. It took three tries and Bluey revving the guts out of the engine to get up the steep incline. A lot of things are done by the swearing method in the outback.

He put the ute in gear and Hakim smiled.

'We go now?'

'We bloody better go now.'

'Bluey?'

'Yeah?' Bluey revved the engine and looked at his personal nemesis.

'We go here.' Hakim pointed to the side of the hill.

'What?'

'We go here.'

Sometimes it takes someone who is not so close to the situation to see a solution. Of course, if you thought about if for a minute or two you might come up with the idea of just driving around the hill, going scrub and off road. It would only add another 8 kilometres of so to the trip and a few centimetres of dust to your general condition.

'Ya mean just off road it?'

'Here.' Hakim pointed and then brought out his dictionary.

'AROUND.' He said the word with rather posh vowels.

'Around.' Bluey frowned.

'Around. Jolly good.'

Bluey sat back and tipped his hat and scratched his bald head.

'Well I'll be. Strike a light.'

The off-road experience wasn't as scenic, but it did have the added effect of saving a few swear words to add to Hakim's vocabulary.

'Bloody brilliant.' Bluey hit the bitumen on the other side of Plinthe Hill and stopped the car.

'Bloody Brilliant.' Hakim smiled.

Between Plinthe Hill and Waterstones South 100 Acre there is a turn off. It leads to a little-known watering hole affectionately known as Five Mile Drop. This establishment is so far off the map that the publican, Ross Slenski keeps his own rules. A yarn that is often told is that

Slenski is in a witness protection programme and … well you didn't hear it from me.

The Five Mile Drop is about 30 klicks from the turn off, but those 30 klicks are worth the wait.

'We need a break.'

'Break.' Hakim nodded and looked in his dictionary.

'I gotta wet me whistle.'

The beer at Five Mile is kept at a delicate 2 degrees Celsius and when that first one hits the back of your throat you know what heaven tastes like. It can make a grown man weep.

Bluey could almost taste the first beer as he recognised the familiar markers on the roadside. Burnt stump, dead gum tree, Waterstone's broken gate, shot up road sign and there it was in the distance.

'Ya gonna love this.' Bluey put the pedal to the metal and started to drool.

'We are stopping?'

'You bet.'

'This is the big smoke.'

'Nah, this is a little bit of heaven mate. Bloody died and gone to heaven.'

'We are in Heaven.'

'You said it.'

Five Mile Drop watering hole was always a pub; someone had the forethought to recognise a man needs a drink now and again.

It had the bull nose verandah, the bread loaf handrail, the sash windows and a bar made of the finest red mahogany. The polish on the bar was a mirror finish, and the saying was, that you could see your true self in the finish … if you dared to look. The old place could have done with a lick of paint, the windows were perpetually stuck and the white ants had been having three squares a day for the last 50 years, but it was still standing and serving beer at 2 degrees, courtesy of the diesel generator out the back. It was an institution and the regulars reckoned it should be heritage listed.

Bluey drove up and parked. He turned to Ralph and gave him a stern talking to.

'Now don't be goin' an' getting any ideas.' Blue tapped the glove compartment. 'Keep out, ya hear me.' Ralph looked out of the driver's window, his face looked like he wasn't listening.

'Shout?' Hakim said.

'A'right.' Blue led the way.

Ross Slenski had a healthy relationship with body hair. It was virtually all over the man, knuckles included. He was broad in the shoulders, a neck that looked like a pylon for the Sydney Harbour Bridge and three gold teeth.

'Is that you Blue?'

'Slenski.' Blue hopped up on a bar stool and pulled Hakim to the next one in line.

'He's me mate.'

'Fair 'nuff.' Slenski cast his critical eye over Hakim.

'Waddleitbe?'

'Cold.'

Slenski pulled a beer and Bluey watched as the head settled.

'An 'im?'

'Same.'

'Wrap ya laughin' gear around this. Cheers mate.' Bluey held his beer aloft and then went to heaven. He closed his eyes and poured the amber liquid down his neck like he was dousing a bush fire on the back lot. He opened his eyes and noticed Hakim was still at it.

'Drink up.' Hakim sipped.

'He sick or summit?'

'Nah.'

'Foreign eh?'

'Yeah.'

'One of them foreign types eh?'

'Yeah.'

Although Slenski wasn't averse to foreign types, he was one himself after all, he liked to think he had bypassed the 'new Australian' trope and gone straight to Ocker the minute he stepped from the boat to the dock.

'Takes all sorts.' He poured another two. The first went down like mother's milk and Bluey relaxed to survey the punters at the bar.

Russ, Flanno and Mick were holding up the bar.

'Bloody foreigners.' Russell Spaulding sniggered behind his beer.

'What's that?'

'I said bloody wogs over here takin' our jobs.' Russ stood on his high moral ground (which was about as high as a bar stool) as the clientele laughed so hard Flanno actually fell off his bar stool.

'Russ, ya drongo. You never done a day's work in ya life.' Flanno turned to the few souls propping up the bar, 'Russ couldn't work if ya wound him up,' and then he laughed 'till he got the stitch.

'Couldn't pull the cotton wool out of an Asprin bottle,' Mick suggested.

'Couldn't work in an iron lung,' Bluey added his favourite. They all had a laugh about that one.

Russ shrunk with every disparaging remark.

'He's me mate right.' Bluey gave a steely stare in Russell's direction.

'Right.' Russ said and supped his beer. 'Just sayin'.'

'Well, shut it.' Slenski polished the bar.'

'All I'm sayin' is that some wogs, sometimes, in some places, take some jobs from some Aussies. That's all I'm sayin'.'

'He's Bluey's mate. He's no wog.'

'Wog?' Hakim asked.

'He's from bloody I-ran.' Bluey said.

'Wog land.' Russell found some Dutch courage.

'He's from I-ran didn't you hear the man.' Slenski waded into the debate.

'Yes. I am from bloody Iran.'

'Wog in a dress.'

'Say that again and you're gonna regret it.' Bluey stood up and hitched up his shorts.

'Yeah. You and who's army?' Russell hopped off his bar stool and stood his ground.

'Just try it mate.'

'All talk mate.'

'Bollocks.' Bluey danced about a bit. 'You wanna a bit of biffo eh?'

'Bring it on.' Russell put up his fists in a show of manliness. That Russell was about a head height smaller than Blue and had as much muscle mass as a plucked chook it didn't look an even match, not by a long shot.

The regulars watched as things were tense. No-one actually connected, but there was a lot of bluff and bluster. A lot of would've, could've, should've.

The regulars, Flanno, Russ and Mick were the type of blokes that were commonly known as gunna men. I'm gunna, just as soon as I get 'round to it, one of these days.

Russ started to recount –the number of times he nearly knocked a bloke for six, the time he almost killed a man; 'if ya could've run in the same direction as him,' Mick said.

69

And the fight he avoided when the coppers pulled him off a bloke.

'Youze was flat out like a lizard drinkin' Russ.' Flanno said.

'Ah, ya weren't there, whaddayouknow.'

'I was there.'

'Weren't.'

'Was.'

'Weren't.'

Flanno went back to his drink. He winked at Bluey and Hakim and mouthed the word, 'was.'

Any witness would have picked Russ out in a line up with their eyes shut.

He was short, almost bald except for the one concession to getting that way, the scrap of a ponytail that grew out of the back of his neck and looked more like an attempt at the Guinness Book of records to be a hairdresser's worst nightmare. It hung like a dead rat's tail down his back. Russell's other attributes sunk as low as a rusty earring in his left lobe, 2 missing teeth and a fading tattoo that the bar regulars took bets on whether it would fade away to a smudge or get swallowed by wrinkly skin. Russ said it was a bikie gang tat, but the odds on that truism were very long.

'Well are ya drinkin' or what?' Slenski waited with two fresh glasses.

'Same again.' Bluey sat down and picked at the pick and mix on the bar. The peanuts were past their use by date when man first walked on the moon and the pretzels were a dentists nightmare – or a holiday in Fiji – depending on his hourly rate.

'So where ya headed Blue?' Flanno asked.

'We are going to the big smoke.' Hakim offered.

'The big smoke eh?'

'Yeah, me mum's crook.'

'She is crook.' Hakim echoed.

'Crikey.'

'Yeah.' Blue said.

'Crikey,' Hakim said and nodded.

'What's his story,' Flanno hoiked his thumb in the direction of Hakim.

Three delicious cold beers put Bluey in that expansive mood again. He nodded for another refill and made himself comfortable.

'Well I got a phone call.' He began at the beginning.

There was the bit about the false teeth, the internet, the meeting with Gordie,

'Gordie Gordonson. How's he doin'?' Flanno asked.

'Good, all good.'

'Good ol' Gordie Gordonson.'

'And Abdul was just standin' there and get this, he thought he was going to New Bloody Zealand.'

'New bloody Zealand.' Hakim said and smiled.

'Ya bloody in Oz-trail-li-aaaa.' Russell said.

'Yes, Oz-trail-li-aaaa, mate.' Hakim nodded.

Bluey didn't miss anything as he ranged over the footy match, the fixing of the ute and then he arrived at Plinthe Hill.

'Bloody hill.' Mick said.

'Too right. Bloody bugger of a hill.' Flanno agreed.

'So, we're at the parking spot, ya know the one?'

They all nodded.

'An Abdul here goes to bleed the lizard.'

'I am bleeding the lizard.' Hakim said, then added, 'I see a bloody big one.'

'Nothin' like a bit o' braggin' mate.' Mick patted Hakim on the back.

'Arright,' Blue choked back a laugh.

71

So, it's a King Brown. A bloody big bugger too and that mongrel of a dog, Ralph thinks he's game for a go.'

The crowd hung off Bluey's every word.

'Bluey saved my life.' Hakim had been practicing the phrase for this very moment.

'Nah.' Bluey blushed. 'Just shot the bugger.'

'A bloody big one.' Hakim added for effect.

The crowd sat back satisfied.

'But that's not the end of it.' Bluey pushed his hat back.

'Abdul here says to me when I'm contemplatin' going up Plinthe Hill, he says all casual like, why don't we go 'round.'

The men sat like stunned mullets.

It was certainly a talking point -if they were talking. The very idea was novel and new. It catapulted Hakim into genius status at the bar.

'Ya kiddin' me.' Mick said.

'Nah.' Bluey grabbed some peanuts and shoved then in his mouth.

'Which way?' Flanno wanted to know the details.

'Around.'

'Oh.' Flanno nodded.

'Ya can't just go 'round.' Russ said.

'We did.' Blue slapped Hakim on the back. Bloody only added 'bout 8 klicks to the whole thing.

'8?' Russ asked.

'8.' Blue slapped the bar.

Blue and Hakim finished their beers and basked in the afterglow.

'Well we gotta get crackin'.'

'Yes, we gotta get crackin'.' Hakim said.

If there was a policeman available he would certainly have brought out a blow in the bag and I'll escort you to the watch house invitation for Bluey.

As it was, the nearest policeman was at the bar. Brian Flannagan aka Flanno was the nearest thing to the law and he was off duty.

As Hakim and Blue left the bar the talk was still about how Blue went *around* Plinthe Hill. Wonders will never cease. If Banjo Patterson was at the bar, all felt sure there'd be a poem written before closing time.

Around, who'd've thunk it! All they needed now was a word to rhyme with Plinthe.

B luey took a deep breath.
       'I drive?' Hakim asked.
'Nah, she'll be right.'
'Bluey?'
'A'right.' Bluey handed over the keys to his mate and they changed seats.

Now any normal person would just hop out of the car and walk around to the other side. When you have had 8 beers between you on an Arnold hamburger the chances of being called normal are about as slim as a donkey winning the Melbourne Cup.

Hakim began by climbing over the gear stick and getting his trousers caught. Bluey decided to squeeze between Hakim and dashboard and the redundant air conditioning button caught his pocket and pulled straight out of the dash.

'Bugger.' Bluey's shirt rode up as he wrestled with his shorts.

Add a dog to the mix and things were about as abnormal as they come. Ralph thought it was a game. He hurdled into the ute and jumped around excited at the prospect of fun. That he had found a bit of roadkill while the fellas were in the bar only added to the mayhem.

It looked like a game of 1970's twister without the fun.

Bluey plopped down into the passenger seat and wiped the sweat from his face.

'Bugger eh?'

'Bugger.' Hakim pushed Ralph away and acquainted himself with the gear stick, the ignition key and the dash.

'I am good with this.' Hakim giggled. Why he thought he'd be any better at driving with 4 schooners in his gut than Blue was the nature of alcohol. It lends itself to all sorts of shenanigans.

'Ya a'right?'

'I am good. I am taxi driver.'

'Right o.' Bluey pushed Ralph to one side and then noticed the teeth marks on the glove compartment knob. He gave Ralph a withering stare.

'Git, ya stink.' Ralph gave his loving master a lick, then sat still and stared ahead.

Anyone familiar with the geography of the world will know that some countries drive on the right, others on the left. It plays havoc with the makers of automobiles, and can be quite disconcerting to foreigners, Iranians included.

Hakim frowned, and concentrated on the road as he put the ute in gear and planted his foot on the accelerator.

The car lurched and stopped, aka stalled.

'I am good.'

'Yeah.' Bluey wiped his brow.

Hakim tried again with more success and the ute took off in a cloud of dust. The wide, empty graded road offered no helpful hints as to which side of the road was the right side, or the wrong side. Hakim took up the habit of a lifetime. FYI, in Iran they drive on the right. So did Hakim.

As the afternoon warmed up to a pleasant 38 degrees in the shade, Bluey began to sweat.

He didn't feel so good. The combination of beer, heat, roadkill and stale peanuts was enough to make anyone feel a little piqued.

When you leave Five Mile Drop there are two ways out. You can go due west and loop back to the 100 acre or you can try your luck with the graded road heading east. The East is quicker, but a bone shaker.

For those who don't know the delights of a graded dirt road the merits are few and far between. A grader, sometime before 1963 might have come through and smoothed the road of lumps and bumps. This is followed by a roller whose sole purpose is to create lumps and bumps. The result is a road with soft patches, hard patches and gravel that resembles marbles. Throw in a few double-bogies with a tonnage that will never get near a weighbridge and the road gets what are affectionately known as corrugations. These are about 50 centimetres apart and are designed to knock your backbone off kilter, ruin your suspension and give your bladder a run for its money. Of course, if you have had beer and peanuts, it's pretty obvious you will need to get rid of the excesses of your hedonistic lifestyle after about 20 minutes.

Hakim took the road East and about 20 minutes in, give or take a minute he stopped the car as Bluey threw open the door and headed for the bush – the only one.

Ralph, being the inquisitive dog he was, followed.

There was a lot of noise, a bit of swearing, but eventually the equilibrium in Bluey's gut was restored.

He came back to the car wiping his mouth.

'Hurled. Bloody feel ok now though.'

It is one of those things. No-one can go past a cow without declaring to those in the car that there is a cow. No-one can throw up without announcing to the present company that they have hurled, chucked up, driven the porcelain bus, chundered or come back for seconds.

'You want?' Hakim offered a 'refreshing' mint.

'Ta.' Bluey took the offering and sat down.

Ralph came back licking his lips.

'Ya shittin' me. Ya dirty bugger.' Blue looked at his mutt. As I mentioned, Ralph may be smart but he was a dog after all.

All three sat in the car and chewed mints as Ralph, aside from smelling like roadkill now had the breath of a public toilet floor.

'Better get crackin'.' Bluey burped and hung out of the window.

Hakim put the old ute into gear and they were off … again.

'Aaaaarrrrreee, yyyyoooooouuu gggoooooddddd nnooowwww?' Hakim said as the corrugations juddered through his system.

'Yeeeeaaaaahh.' Blue dribbled out the window, taking the place of Ralph.

Around the 50 kilometre mark the grader had given up and gone home and the road turned to tarmac. The black top was smooth, straight and wide. The white lines were perfectly marked, the verge graded to the perfection of a French chateau garden and the reflectors in the centre line were new. It was an eerie experience to see a beautiful bit of roadbuilding out the middle of nowhere. It was as if the lads knew the supervisor was on his way and pulled their finger out. That, or the apprentice was trying to pass his last exam.

'This is good.' Hakim put his foot down and relished the feel of the open road.

It was all going great guns until a road-train the size of a … well train, loomed ahead. It wouldn't have been a problem except they were both intent on sharing the same side of the road.

'Bloody hell.' Bluey woke up to the sounding of the MAC's horn, or it could have been the seven trumpets of apocalypse, he was in a bit of a panic.

'Abdul,' Bluey wrenched the wheel and they ended up skidding on the verge as the MAC thundered past, the driver giving a little more than the country wave. He also said something that might make a lip reader blush.

'Jeezzzzus.' Bluey sat back and wiped the sweat from his eyes. Ralph climbed over Bluey, thinking it was time for a stretch.

'Git.' Ralph jumped out of the ute and meandered into the bush.

'What the f'ing hell happened?'

'This man, he is crazy.' Hakim pointed to the road.

Bluey, now stone cold sober dug into the back of his brain and came up with the answer.

'Abdul,'

'Yes?'

'In Straya we drive on the left.' Blue pointed to the road and made the universal sign for driving by gripping Hakim's collar and shaking the living daylights out of him.

'Ya coulda kill us.'

'You save my life.'

'Ah, git outta here.'

'You save my life.' Hakim leaned over to hug Blue.

'Hang on a minute.' Bluey moved away.

'You save my life.'

'A'right. A'right.' Blue held out his hand for a handshake. 'I ain't gay or anything. Ya know that don't cha.'

'Yes, I am gay.' Hakim smiled and laughed and winked.

'Got that.' Blue opened the car door and whistled for Ralph.

'We gotta get crackin'.

'Crackin',' Hakim nodded.

'I betta drive eh?'

They changed places with the benefit of hindsight and walked around the car.

Blue looked at the petrol gauge and made a calculation.

The next petrol station was two hours away. They had just enough … or he could detour over the worst road ever to be called a road, in fact it was called the ball buster track, and reach Bruno's truckstop at 60 clicks.

Bluey put the choice to Hakim.

'They got beds and showers at Bruno's. The men were under no illusions that they were beginning to stink worse than Ralph, and that was saying something.

What had started out as a 10 hour trip in the same underwear was rapidly turning into a marathon, and Bluey knew he didn't have the stamina to sit in the same clothes for more than three days without getting a rash.

Once, out west, when they were fencing his swag fell off the back of the truck and he lost the lot. No-one knows better than Bluey the perils of staying in your jocks more than three days. The doc said he needed to administer the cream for two bloody weeks. The ribbing from Cricket, Johnno and Nev was more than he could stand.

'We could, ya know, just kinda, get petrol and stuff.'

'Yes.'

'A'right.' Bluey hit the road.

The Lot 42b track or BB track as the locals like to call it, starts at a stand of dead eucalyptus trees. It is nothing more than a track with two ruts for wheels and about metre high grass in the middle. If a vehicle can traverse the track then the makers of suspension kits know they are on a winner. Blue stopped at the dead trees.

'Are ya game?'

'We are playing a game?' Hakim asked.

'Nah. Are ya up for it? Ya know, are ya ready.'

'I am ready.' Hakim looked at the bush ahead. Ralph whimpered.

They headed off-road as the sun began to make its journey to the horizon.

'Should be there before dark.' Blue said with little conviction. The Ball Buster track had acquired legend status as people were stranded, broke axels, smashed wheels and hit roos

'Watchout for roos.'

'Watchout for roos?' Hakim shrugged.

'Yeah, roos. Ya know, kang -a- bloody-roos.'

'Ah, kang-a-bloody-roos.' Hakim nodded. If the Australian government has done one thing worth noting, it is the dissemination of information linking Australia and the kangaroo. A tourist might not know where Oz is, but they know what a kangaroo looks like. It might have something to do with the 1970's programme called Skippy, but that would be giving the television too much credit for the dissemination of information.

'I know this kang -a-bloody-roo.'

'Yeah, well watch out for 'em. They got a death wish.'

They hit the track, the first dip a doozy that made Ralph land on Bluey lap and get tangled up in the steering wheel.

'Git.'

Ralph git.

The only saving grace of the trip was the sun setting behind them. There is nothing worse than driving into a setting sun. The ute bounced in and out of ruts, holes and over lumps.

'I am watching for kang-a-bloody-roos.' Hakim said as he hung on to the hand hold above his head.

'Nice one.' Bluey's guts was jammed between the wheel and his back bone at a particularly savage dip. They carried on bouncing around in the cab when Hakim shouted,

'Stop.'

Blue jammed on the breaks and swivelled his head about.

'What?'

'I see.' Hakim pointed to a mob of kangaroos to their right.

'Bloody Nora.'

'Kang-a-bloody-roos.' Hakim pointed like a tourist.

'Yeah. Well that's the buggers. Watch out eh.'

'I'm watching.'

The roos stood to attention at the passing of the ute. Seen one, seen 'em all, and went back to grazing.

The track at 30 clicks passes over a sandy depression known as the bog; Aussies most of the time call it like it is. In Australia you don't need mud to get stuck, sand will do the trick. Blue and Hakim stopped and looked at the sand ahead in the fading light.

'She's a bugger a'right.'

'Bugger.'

'You said it.' Blue knew the perils of sand. He revved the engine and took the bog at speed. A ute may have the pedigree of the workhorse, but even a workhorse can't perform miracles. It was a given Bluey wouldn't make it. The ute got stuck.

'Bugger.'

'Bugger.' Hakim said.

There are many and various ways to get out of a bogged situation. Swearing helps, but putting something for grip under the wheels is the tried and trusted method. He got

Hakim foraging for branches, wood, sticks and shrubs and as the sun casts it last glorious rays across the sunburnt landscape the pair inched forward on their raft of scrubwood, Hakim replacing the wood from the back of the wheels to the front.

'Ya right there.' Bluey yelled as they neared the end of the bog.

'I am good.' Hakim said through gritted teeth. His back was killing him and his calf muscles were ready to throw in the towel. Walking in sand is more than an aerobic workout.

The front wheels finally found purchase on hard ground and Blue gave the ol' ute one final kick and she leapt onto terra firma.

'Rippa.' He honked the horn which set Ralph barking in excitement.

'C'on, whatcha waitin' for?' Blue thumped the side of the car door.

Hakim staggered to the ute and fell into the seat next to Ralph.

'I … am,' he huffed and puffed. 'I am …'

'Rooted?' Blue offered the adjective.

'Rooted.' Hakim didn't know what it meant, but it would do as he tried to regain his breath.

'Well, we're nearly there now.' Blue put his foot down and they bounced and bumped their way to Bruno's, the headlights never actually hitting the road ahead as the car lurched from one swerving corner, pot hole and ditch to the next.

The truck-stop in the distance lit up the sky. It had flashing lights, spotties, neon signs and strobes. The men fixed their eyes on the Mecca for truckies and didn't take they gaze off it until Blue cut the engine in the parking bay.

'We are here?'

'Bloody oath we are here.' Blue licked his lips in expectation of a cold drink, a shower – shampoo provided, and a bed for the night with clean sheets and air conditioning that only had one setting - cold.

Hakim swatted at a mozzie and fidgeted with his suitcase.

'Nah, don't worry mate. I'll fix ya up. Ya can settle later.'

'Pardon?'

'My shout.'

'SHOUT.' Hakim smiled.

'Yeah.' Blue pulled his wallet from his back pocket. 'My shout. Ya got us outta the bog and that's gotta be worth a bit of tucker and a bed.' Blue slapped Hakim on the back.

'C'on. Let's get inta it.

Bruno's truckstop was a place where men are men and the shampoo is free. Bruno and his wife, Maria were industrious, and had made the truckstop into a sort of home away from home for truckies and wayward souls who travel the outback.

He was short, she shorter, and both had the girth that cheese, wine, cheese, chips, cheese, beer, cheese and cake can produce in 60 years. They also knew all the gossip so it was no surprise that by the time Bluey got to the counter Maria was already asking about his ol' mum.

'She's-a crook eh?'

'Yeah. Crook.'

'She's-a in 'ospital?'

'Yeah.' Bluey nodded.

'Crook.' Hakim added.

'You-a going to-a town.'

'Yeah.' Blue pulled out his wallet. 'We're wantin' a room, ya know, a bed for the night eh?'

'I only gott-a one room. You know how it is eh?'

'Jeez.' Blue looked at Hakim.

'Now ya know I'm not gay or anythin'.'

'I am gay.' Hakim nodded and smiled.

'Yeah. You gotta sleep over there.' Blue pointed to the single bed, an' I'm here,' he pointed to the double bed.'

'Ok, Bluey.' Hakim put his suitcase down on the bed. 'Ralph?'

'He's in the ute.' Blue had found an old hessian sack and made Ralph comfortable in the ute with the window down. There is only so much dog smell one can stand after a scrub up and free shampoo.

'I'll go first.' Blue took the towel shaped like a seashell from the end of his bed and headed for a tub. 'Nuthin' like a bit of a scrub up.'

'Ok. I'm rooted.' Hakim said.

Blue came out looking fresh. He'd washed his smalls in the shower and lay down on the bed with the towel wrapped around his midriff.

'Your turn.'

Hakim went in and found Bluey jocks hanging off the curtain rail. He gently pushed them to one side and got down to business.

With a towel wrapped around his midriff he too lay down on his bed and revelled in the feeling of being clean.

'Ripper init?'

'Ripper.' The men lay back and the gentle smell of lavender and lily of the valley wafted over the pair.

'Bloody good to be alive.'

'Yes. Jolly good.'

Ralph scratched at the window and whimpered.
'Git.' Bluey said from his bed.
'Ralph, he wants a scrub up.' Hakim said from his bed.
'Nah.'
'Bluey, Ralph he stink.'
'You're tellin' me.' Bluey grabbed the remote control for the television. 'You got tele in I-ran Abdul?'
'Pardon?'
'You got the tele in I-ran? Ya know, the idiot box.' Bluey pointed to the television set high on the wall. He tried the remote, but it didn't work and there was no way he could reach the knobs near the ceiling. There was a sneaking suspicion that Bruno didn't actually want people to use the tele for the advertised *free* satellite TV. It looked good on the neon sign anyway.
'Yes, we have.' Hakim said.
'Ya reckon you'll go back?' Bluey mimed going back to Iran on an aeroplane.
Hakim shook his head. 'No.'
'Ya could bring ya family here ya know. Out to Straya.'
'Pardon?'
'Ya family. Mum, Dad, the whole bloody lot of 'em. They'd be safe here.' Blue picked up the dictionary and got his message across.
'Yes. I like this.' Hakim nodded. 'I try. I get taxi. I make dollars.'

'Yeah, that's the way. Get a job first.'

'You have job?'

'I got a job mate. Maybe I could get ya fixed up, ya know somethin' to get ya goin'.'

'Fixed up.'

'Look, I'll see what I can do eh?' Blue smiled then they heard Ralph at the door.

'Bluey, Ralph?'

'A'right, a'right.'

'I can do.'

'Knock ya self out.' Bluey picked up the room delivery menu and squinted at the delights.

'You eat pizza?'

'Pizza?'

'Ok then.' Blue picked up the phone and asked for two large pizzas with the lot. Bruno and Maria weren't called Pizigliano for nothing.

Hakim called Ralph into the room and coaxed him into the shower cubical.

It was a bonding moment as Hakim gently played warm water over Ralph and took advantage of the free shampoo. Ralph sat still and if the adoration in his eyes was any indication he was 'in' the moment and loving it.

Bluey snored as Hakim made Ralph into something more than a working dog with a nose for roadkill.

When he'd finished Ralph smelt like lily of the valley and lavender and his coat had a gloss that might have won first prize. Hakim gave him a rub down and their moment was interrupted by a knock at the door.

'Eh?' Blue sat up.

'Peeetsah.'

'A'right.' Blue adjusted his towel and opened the door just as Hakim opened the bathroom door.

It was one of those scenes that fiction writers call suspense.

Hakim looked at the delivery lad, Luigi. Luigi looked at Ralph, Bluey looked at Hakim and Ralph ran to the bed and jumped up to make himself comfortable. The realisation that they had a dog in the room and that said dog could get them kicked out – without their pizza and they'd be wearing wet jocks, which can inflict a rash worse than 3 days continuous and that they'd probably get banned – and the news'd travel faster than a welfare payment to the pub ran through Bluey's mind. He may not run fast, but he's good in a crisis.

'Seein' eye dog – bugger's blind as a bat.'

Luigi looked at Ralph and back to Hakim. Bluey ran to his wallet and whipped out a $20.

'I found it, wondered if it was yours?'

'Yeah, all good.' Luigi smirked and put the pizzas down on the small kitchen table. He snatched the twenty quicker than a kookaburra's swoop on a BBQ and left.

'That was bloody close.' Blue looked at Ralph who was walking around in circles trying to decide which side of the bed was his.

'Git.'

Ralph git.

The pizzas were the size of hubcaps, one each. Blue licked his lips. He wasn't the only one as Ralph crept up to the table.

'We are all mates eh?'

'You said it.' Blue handed Hakim a slice of pizza.

'Mate.

'Mate.'

Ralph whimpered in anticipation.

Hakim looked at the tele.

'I can try.' He climbed up on his chair and pressed some knobs and the screen burst into life … if that's what you call two channels to choose from – one showing the Lion King, the other Love Actually.

'I know this,' Hakim pointed to the Lion King. He hopped down and made himself comfortable on his bed, the only problem being he couldn't actually see the tele.

Bluey had settled himself down on his bed, his pizza on his lap, Ralph sitting on his feet ready to be entertained.

'A'right.' Blue let Hakim sit next to him. 'I'm not bloody gay, ya know that right.'

'I am gay, always gay.' Hakim gave a laugh and put his pizza on his lap.

If I told you that two grown men were sitting in their bath towels, eating pizzas the size of hub caps and singing The Circle of Life you wouldn't believe me. Sometimes you just need to take my word for it.

Blue fell asleep and his pizza slipped to the floor. Ralph patience paid off as he finished the lot and settled down on Bluey's feet.

Hakim only made it to Akuna Matata and he slipped into the land of nod.

The men were woken by Ralph scratching at the door and looking a bit frantic.

'What the …' Blue rubbed his eyes and sat up. It took a moment or two, but when he re-joined the land of the living he noticed Hakim waking up next to him and they were both in a state of undress.

Hakim looked over to Bluey and then to Ralph who was scratching at the door. There is always that moment of indecision. He couldn't get out of bed, being nude as he was. He hunted around for his towel and decided a pizza box would do.

It is a delicate operation to cover your dignity while getting out of bed and walking to the door. It requires some quick manoeuvres with greasy cardboard. Hakim scooted to the door and opened it for Ralph who shot out and found a tree.

'Shut the bloody door.' Blue said as he pulled the sheet up to his neck.

Hakim backed over to the bathroom and slipped inside. He came out dressed and ready for the day.

'I am jolly good.'

'A'right.' Bluey said. 'Let's get this straight. Ya know I'm not gay or anything poofterish.'

'Poofterish?' Hakim frowned.

'Ya know. Like sissy. Like being extra friendly with ya mates.'

Hakim shook his head. He fetched his dictionary and gave it to Bluey. Blue looked up homosexual and pointed.

'It's gay. Ya know all girlie like and well a poofta.' Blue threw his arms about from the bed and acted like a silly school girl, albeit with a bit of Pricilla Queen on the desert thrown in and blew Hakim at kiss.

Hakim backed away. His eyes grew wide and he sat down on his bed and rubbed the stubble on his chin.

'Poofta?'

'Yeah, that's right. Poofta.'

Hakim looked anywhere but at Blue.

'Ok,' he said in a measured tone. Now they were both holding the wrong end of the stick.

It took a bit of side stepping, but Blue and Hakim made themselves presentable, after Bluey had availed himself of the free shampoo ... again.

They made their way to the restaurant for breakfast. The Pizigliano's had the business acumen to forgo the usual kettle, instant coffee (which tastes like sock washing water) the tea bags (which resemble a bag of dust) and the three ubiquitous sugar cubes. If you want-a break-a-fast you-a need to-a buy it.

Hakim looked at the fare under hot lights. Sausages and bacon rashers - dripping in fat, chips - dripping in fat, eggs that looked like their rubber equivalent and all manner of deep-fried food.

'Got any toast?' Blue asked.

'We got-a toast.' Maria nodded then pulled two slices of bread from the packet and put them under the grill.

'Whatcha havin'?' Blue asked Hakim. He shrugged. It all looked a bit too greasy for breakfast when you are accustomed to coffee -strong and black, figs, honey and yogurt, then ending with one of your mother's delicious sesame treats.

'Coffee?' Hakim asked.

'We got-a coffee.' Maria busied herself with the cappuccino machine.

'Expresso?'

Maria suddenly looked up. Here was a man after her own heart. An expresso drinker no less, way out here in the middle of nowhere. She smiled.

'You know-a your coffee,' she said.

'Expresso,' Hakim nodded and flashed his winning smile.

Nothing was too good for the couple, Maria decided.

'Sit, sit.' She ushered the men to the prime table near the window.

'I bring-a your break -a-fast.'

Bluey sat down and fiddled with the salt and pepper.

'Ya drink coffee eh?'

'Yes. Coffee.' Hakim said. 'Iran we all drink coffee.'

'Ya eat toast?' Blue took the plate from Maria.

'This?' Hakim pointed.

'Yeah, toast 'n' vegemite.'

'Vegemite?'

Of course, anyone who had access to the internet knows the perils of offering vegemite to a foreigner. This black spread is peculiar to Australian tastes. It's super salty, looks like tar and has a tang that is hard for a non-native to put their finger on. Aussies are brought up on the stuff from the moment they can chew.

Blue spread his toast and gave a slice to Hakim.

'G'on, give it a go.'

Hakim looked at the conglomeration of melted butter and vegemite on something that passed as bread.

'Ok mate.' He took a bite and chewed with a forced smile. His expresso arrived and Maria hovered for a verdict.

Hakim sipped the deliciously strong coffee made with Italian knowhow.

'Rippa.' He smiled at Maria and she melted and went all coy.

'You like-a.'

'I like-a.' Hakim held the old woman's hand, then kissed it.

'Gracia.' Maria blushed and bustled away.

Hakim looked at the vegemite and toast.

'Ya like it?' Blue asked.

'I like-a.' Hakim closed his eyes and revelled in his expresso.

The moment was interrupted by Maria bearing two plates of breakfast. She put them down on the table and stood over the men.

'Eat.' It wasn't a request. 'Gratuito,' she added.

'Huh?'

'Free.' Maria stood over Hakim and watched him like a hawk.

When you're not really in the mood for a big breakfast and a little Italian lady is hovering the only thing to do is eat.

Hakim and Bluey ate, it was free after all.

Sausages, bacon, eggs, chicko rolls, chips and hash browns were washed down with coffee and tea. It was a mammoth effort for the men. After all, they had devoured most of a hubcap of pizza each just 12 hours before.

Blue sat back and burped.

'S'cuse.' Blue rubbed his belly. 'Stuffed.'

'Stuffed.' Hakim relaxed and let his jaw go slack. They sat back, replete.

'All good?' Maria came over for the plates.

'Bloody rippa.' Bluey said.

'Magnifique.' Hakim said and kissed Maria's hand. This time Bruno saw the exchange and decided enough was enough. Making up to his wife was one thing, a free breakfast was taking the friendship too far.

'Eh?' Bruno put his hands on his hips.

'Mate.' Blue burped.

'Mate.' Hakim stood up and towered over Bruno.

'You outta here.'

'Just leavin'.' Blue stood up and pulled Hakim to the door.

They staggered out into the blazing sun and squinted.

'C'on.' Blue led the way to the ute.

The day was turning into a stinker. A stinker in Aussie terms is anything over 38 degrees in the shade. Hakim and Bluey looked at the pale blue sky, the horizon and the black road ahead.

'Gonna be a bloody stinker.'

'Stinker.' Hakim nodded and pushed Ralph away. Ralph had the crazy idea that Hakim was his pack masters and he couldn't get close enough to the top man. Ralph lay his paw on Hakim's leg and looked adoringly in Hakim's direction his tongue dripping onto the seat.

The ute's cab wasn't the most pleasant place to be regardless of lily of the valley and lavender. The heat wafted into the cab, Ralph was panting, and no matter how much free shampoo one has availed oneself of, it doesn't take the place of deodorant. The day was certainly a stinker. Ralph took a look at Blue and then at the knob on the glove compartment. He knew he was in trouble. Blue took one look at the chewed knob and gave his dog a stare that to Ralph meant he was in big trouble.

'Ya mongrel. Look what ya done.' Blue pointed to the knob that was a shadow of it's former self. Ralph tried to look out of the window, anywhere but at Blue.

'Ya a bloody pest. Ya not getting' 'em.' He pushed the knob and tried to lock the compartment that housed Bill's teeth. Ralph whimpered and climbed on Hakim's lap.

'Ya gotta watch Ralph. He's a cunning bastard.'
'I will watch.' Hakim pushed Ralph off his lap.

Bluey started the ute and fixed his eye on the road ahead. He burped.

'We're not far now. 'bout 200 to go.' He drew the number in the dust on the dashboard.

'To the big smoke?'

'Yeah, that's right.' Bluey took a last look at the truck-stop, burped, and turned onto the bitumen for the last 200 kilometres.

They drove for about 40 minutes when Bluey began to squirm.

'You are ok?' Hakim noticed Bluey wasn't quite right.

'Yeah.' Blue burped and blew out a breath and drove another 30 clicks.

A stink invaded the cabin. Blue looked at Ralph. Hakim looked at Bluey, and Ralph whimpered and tried to hang out the window.

'Ralph?' Hakim enquired.

'Bloody mongrel.' Blue looked at his dog, but as anyone knows, trying to pin a fart on the dog when he is the innocent party is all about keeping a straight face.

Blue cracked a smile.

'Bluey?' Hakim asked as he tried to push Ralph to one side to get to the window.

'Sorry mate. Just couldn't help it.' Blue shrugged and smiled. 'It's all that bloody food.'

Hakim began to laugh.

'It's your bloody fault mate. You an' your bloody expresso.'

'Bloody expresso.' Hakim hooted and wiped the tears from his eyes.

'Bloody expresso.' Bluey said again and they convulsed in laughter. Naturally when you are laughing, a fart is about the hardest thing to keep behind the curtain.

Bluey let rip and Ralph actually tried to climb out of the window.

'Sorry mate. Just dropped a bomb.'

'Bomb?' Hakim's eyes widened. 'This is very funny.'

'Too right. Ya tellin' me.'

'Your bomb is killing me,' Hakim said through gaffawfs.

He rummaged for a 'refreshing mint' and popped two then gave one to Ralph. Bluey needed more than a refreshing mint, he needed a cork – or about 20 minutes with a Popular Mechanics and a roll of triple ply toilet paper. The men giggled for another 10 clicks and slowly regained some sense of propriety, although every time Hakim said bomb it went off with a bang and they giggled some more.

There is a public convenience about 70 km from the big smoke at Strickland Flats. It is one of those civic pride places that has shiny taps that only give you three seconds of water, stainless steel mirrors that contort your features so you might seek a doctor's opinion once at your destination and toilets that forgo the usual configuration and don't have seats.

Bluey pulled up at the well-appointed carpark with new curbing, saplings growing in concrete and myriad of signs and cut the engine.

'Just nippin' in.' Blue almost ran. Ralph jumped out of the ute and headed for the saplings. Hakim followed Bluey.

I'm not sure about most people, but there is a certain etiquette that is expected when visiting a public toilet.

Bluey threw etiquette out the window. When a man has needs, niceties take second place.

I should explain that Bluey's alimentary tract likes to get the most out of his tucker. He has been known to go three days without so much as a fart. So, when the need arises, he has learned from experience he needs to take the opportunity – it may not come again for some time. Naturally, nothing comes without effort. The doctor had warned Bluey of the perils, but old habits die hard.

Blue sat on the cold stainless steel and the noises emanating could have been from the depths of hell.

There were moans, groans, huff and puff. There were snorts, howls and a few choice swear words.

'Bluey?' Hakim knocked on the cubical door.

'Yeah.' Blue said gripping his knees trying to give birth. 'Ok?'

'Yeah.' Blue went through second stage contractions.

Hakim looked in the mirror and decided he might need to visit a doctor when he got to the big smoke. He didn't look too good. He heard Bluey scream – a low crawling animal scream that was not of this world, and then the toilet flushed.

'Ok?' Hakim saw Bluey walk from the cubical like a conquering hero.

'Bloody rippa.'

'You choke a darkie?'

'Bloody oath.'

'We get cracking now?'

'Too right.' Bluey hitched his shorts and stretched. 'C'on.'

With only 70 kilometres to go Bluey began to think on the logistics.

'Where ya going?'

'Pardon?'

'Where da ya wanna be dropped?' Blue asked. 'Ya know, let off. Address?'

'Ah.' Hakim nodded. He pulled out a bit of paper and handed it over to Bluey.

'This is bloody New bloody Zealand.'

'Yes.'

'Well, ya not gonna get any joy in the big smoke with this,' he handed the paper back. 'Ya better just come to me sister's place. She'll know what to do.'

'Sister.'

'Yeah, ya gonna love her. She's the best cook this side of the black stump.'

'Ah.' Hakim sat back. Apparently Bluey had it all under control.

Bluey drove into the town like a yokel at 40 km/h. The open road is fine, but put more than three cars on the road at the same time and Blue was Mr Careful. He hugged the gutter, he signalled three hundred metres from the corner and crawled up to the traffic lights in first.

'You want me drive?' Hakim knuckles were white with frustration. Taxi drivers know a thing or two about traffic.

'Nah, she's right.' Blue wiped the sweat from his face and hunched over the steering wheel anticipating the next big accident. The roundabout was negotiated with caution bordering on nervous breakdown. (Hakim was gripping the seat so tight his fingers went through the upholstery.)

'Must be rush hour,' he said, although it was 2pm and the hottest part of the day when only those in search of a cold beer or a spare part for an air conditioner were on the road. The big smoke was not that big.

Bluey took the turn into the suburban street and crawled down the road in first gear and pulled up next to a small weatherboard house with a garden that looked like it had been dead before the garden hose was invented.

'This is me sister's place. Gwen. She's married to Lance.'

'Gwen.'

'Yeah.'

'Lance.'

'Yeah.' Blue turned off the engine and wiped his brow, the traffic had taken its toll. He was exhausted.

Gwen was at the door before Bluey was out of the cab. She folded her arms across her copious chest and waited for her brother to make his way to the door.

Gwendolen Cracknell, nee Gaylore was a small, compact stick of dynamite. She could knit you a jumper and bake a cake while hanging out the washing and looking after the home brew before you had time to blink. She had a frizz of red hair that defied anything resembling a style except with a rubber band and a figure that might be described as a barrel. She was also quite single minded about men, dogs, brothers, beer and the neighbours.

'He's not comin' inside.' She pointed in the direction of the ute.

'He's from I-ran.'

'The dog you idiot.' Gwen rolled her eyes.

'Oh.' Bluey loved his sister, but sometimes his love was sorely tested.

'He can stay out back.'

'A'right.' Blue roused Ralph and put him in the backyard then shut the gate.

'C'on.' He waved his arm at Hakim. 'She's won't bite,' he looked at Gwen, 'not yet anyway.'

Hakim straightened himself up, grabbed his suitcase and walked up the garden path.

'I am very pleased to meet you.' He gave a winning smile.

'Getouttahere.' Gwen blushed and took the offered hand. Hakim lingered over the hand and Gwen went to pieces.

'He's nice, eh?'

'Yeah. If ya like that kinda stuff.'

'Like what stuff?' Lance came to the door and looked over Hakim.

'Who's he?'

'Abdul. He's from I-ran. I picked him up.'

'Does he drink beer.'

'I am drinking.' Hakim nodded. 'I am Hakim.'

'Well what are we doin' standin' around.' Lance led the way into the darkened house.

Lance Cracknell wasn't particularly handsome, nor was he hit with an ugly stick. He was Mr Normal. He had a beer muscle that had stopped him seeing his toes for the last twenty years, but he could still tie his shoelaces – if he wore shoes, most days he was in pluggers. He was of average height and you could probably say he was a nice enough bloke. But the one thing that made Lance stand out from the crowd was his hair.

He had, what a barber would call 'the mother of all combovers'. A stupendous combover. Something to write home about.

Some men go bald and don't bat an eyelid. Some men shave off the remaining tufts and leave it to their wives to let them know when it's time to get the mower out again. And then there are those men who remember a time when they had hair and hang onto the past with the tenacity of superglue. (Not that superglue helped keep their hair.)

Lance was a bit vain.

For the uninformed, a combover is that hairstyle that doesn't take too kindly to wind. The wearer grows their hair long on one side of their bald patch and carefully combs the long side over to the short side, covering the empty space in-between. It's pretty obvious, rarely works well and is a devil to keep in place. And it's not fooling anyone – ever!

Lance ran his fingers over his hair, hitched up his shorts and said, 'Bloody stinker of a day eh?'

'Stinker.' Hakim took the cold can of beer and tried to take his eye off Lance's head. It wasn't easy.

'Cheers. Bottoms up mate.' Lance held his beer aloft.

'Mate,' Blue said as he slammed the coldie down his neck. Hakim wasn't far behind as the cold drink took his temperature down a peg or two.

Gwen stood in the doorway and watched the men.

'We were expectin' ya days ago.'

'Yeah. Well I had things to do. Abdul and me had business.'

'Drinkin' business if I know you Blue,' Gwen said. 'Ya want a feed?'

'What ya got?' Bluey nudged Hakim and winked. Hakim slid a little closer to Lance on the three-seater settee; a wink pretty much universal language in the scheme of things.

'You hungry mate?' Gwen smiled at Hakim. 'Does he speak his own lingo or Oztralian?'

'Sort of a bit of both,' Blue said.

'Hun-g-rarrrrry,' Gwen said and mimed eating.

'Just bring somethin'. I told him youze the best cook this side of the black stump anyroads.'

'Oh, Blue.' Gwen swept out of the room and busied herself in the kitchen.

'So, ya heard about Agnes?' Lance asked as he cracked a coldie.

'She's in 'ospital.' Gwen yelled from the kitchen.

'Me mum's a tough ol' bird.'

'Your mother is a bird?' Hakim frowned trying to follow the conversation.

'Nah. She's tough. Ya know, strong.' Blue said.

'Well she's feeling a bit crook just now.' Lance shook his head.

'Crook.' Hakim nodded.

'Yeah, she's gonna be in for a bit after the op the doc said.'

Gwen came in with a big fry-up. 'Git up at the table. I figured you'd be hungry after a long drive.' They followed Gwen to the dining room.

Bluey looked at Hakim. Hakim looked at Bluey and they contemplated the plate of chips, sausages, bacon, eggs, tomato and beans all covered in BBQ sauce.

'Well, whatchawaitin'for? Eat.' Gwen waited for a measure of her endeavours in the kitchen.

Hakim poked at a sausage and then got stuck in. Bluey was slow on the uptake, playing with his beans.

'Got any dead horse Gwen?' Blue sent his sister scurrying into the kitchen. He took the opportunity to open the window and throw some of his meal to Ralph. It didn't take Hakim more than three seconds to follow suit.

'Beaut Gwen,' Blue said as he sat back and licked his lips.

'Crickey, that was quick.' Gwen took their plates. 'Ya wanna cuppa?'

'Yeah.' Blue looked at Hakim, 'Tea? Ya wanna a cupa tea?'

'Tea.'

'Yeah.'

'Yes please.'

'He's very polite innhe.' Gwen said.

'Yeah. Those fellas from I-ran are like that.'

'Where's I-ran then?' Lance came into the dining room.

'Hey Abdul, where's I-ran.' Blue prompted. Hakim looked around the room for an atlas when he spied a smart phone. He grabbed it and typed and a map popped up which he showed the assembled company.

'Oh, there.' Gwen said.

'It's one of them Arabie countries eh?'

'I am taxi driver.'

'Oooo, he speaks a bit-a Ozzie then.' Gwen smiled at Hakim.

'So, what's his story eh?' Gwen put a pot of tea on the table and sat down next to Hakim.

'Well, don't get me wrong or anything, but straight up he's a poofta.'

'Really?'

'Yeah.' Blue smiled at Hakim and winked.

'Poofta.' Hakim said and winked at Bluey.

And then Bluey told them the whole story starting with the phone call. Although Gwen knew that bit, as she was the one making the call, but it's best to get things straight and start at the beginning. He might have left out the bit where they were found in the swag together. He forgot to mention they were in bed together in a hotel room with nothing more than a bath towel between them and he considered telling Gwen about their free breakfast, but decided to err on the side of caution.

Naturally as the yarn progressed the snake was a bit bigger, the fangs a little closer to Hakim's leg, the ball buster track a tad harder and the bog quite a lot deeper. But such is the nature of a good ol' yarn. It's all in the telling.

'He saved my life.' Hakim said and sipped his tea.

'Nah.' Blue blushed. 'I just shot the bastard.'

'I was rooted.'

'Hell's bells.' Gwen said.

Lance was on the edge of his seat. He hadn't had this much excitement since he nearly won a bet on the Melbourne cup.

'So that's about it.' Bluey sat back and the only sound that could be heard as the day slowly ticked down from the 40 degree scorcher was Ralph throwing up in the back yard. Even a dog has his limit.

Agnes Gaylore was one tough ol' bird. She sat up in her hospital bed and watched the tele with the dedication of someone watching for the police at an underage drinking party. She knew all the shows, all the stars, all the gossip and could tell you who was shagging who, if you cared to ask.

She was just getting stuck into Renovator's Dream when Gwen walked in with Lance, Bluey and Hakim.

'G'day mum,' Gwen gave Agnes a peck on the cheek. Agnes waved the affection away, 'just a sec,' she said as she watched paint dry. 'Commercial comin' up.'

They all waited – watching paint dry until the aftershave commercial came on.

'G'day mum.' Blue came in close and gave his ol' mum a kiss on the cheek.

'Bluey.'

'Yeah.' Bluey ran his finger around the collar of the shirt he had borrowed from Lance. It was constricting and felt like it was made of prickles.

'So ya in 'ospital then.'

'Yeah.' Agnes said, keeping an eye on the tele.

'Crook then eh?'

'Yeah, the doc said I need the op.'

'The op?'

Agnes waved the question away as her programme resumed. The paint now dry they all watched as the contestants squabbled over the colour.

At the next three minutes of commercials Lance came into the conversation.

'When's the op Agnes?'

'Doc says tomorra. I'm not s'posed to have anything ta eat or anything.'

Bluey put the bag with chocolates on the floor.

'What's ya problem mum?' Blue asked.

He had to wait until magenta was debated with puce, a runner up in the fashionable end of town before his mum answered.

'Same ol' problem. We all got the same problem Blue.' Agnes gave a knowing look at Bluey. 'Ya a Gaylore and that's a dead cert for piles.'

'Piles.' Bluey tried to steer the conversation away from something he'd rather not discuss.

'I know you got 'em Blue. We all got 'em. Ain't that right Gwen?'

'Yeah. The Gaylore's got 'em all right.'

'We're prone the doc said.' Agnes shushed the crowd as textured rollers were put on show for the contestants. Someone suggested a sponge, someone else a rag. The consensus was that the suede look was effective for the living room.

'I'm just telling ya, is all. Ya need to get 'em checked,' and here Agnes stretched her bony hand and grabbed Bluey forearm, 'before it's too late.' She settled her beady eye on her only son. She then looked at the crowd in the room and saw Hakim standing in the corner watching the tele.

'Who's he?' Agnes pointed.

'That's Abdul, he's me mate.' Blue beckoned Hakim forward.

'This is me mum.'

'The bird?'

'Eh?' Agnes said, then her attention was drawn to the merits of tiles in the bathroom and coloured grout. Hakim had to wait until the Baby wipes commercial came on to be formally introduced.

'I am very pleased to meet you. You are crook?'

'Yeah.'

Hakim took Agnes's hand and held it to his chest. 'I am hoping you can not be crook.'

'He's nice eh?'

'That's what I said. He's nice eh?'

'For a poof.'

'Eh?'

Agnes didn't hear the explanation as she was caught up in the debate on a mixter tap versus retro hot and cold on a blue porcelain basin. The plinth versus double sinks was the killer question.

After the antacid commercial Agnes waved her visitors away. She needed to get ready for Game of Thrones.

'We'll come by tomorra after the op.' Gwen said as she made her way to the door. 'I'll ring.'

'Not before three.' Agnes said. 'Days of their Lives finishes at three.' Such was the heady, almost dizzying full social calendar of Agnes Gaylore.

'She looked well enough.' Gwen said in the car on the way home.

'Yeah.' Blue sat back and offered a choccie to Hakim and Lance.

'Oooo, mint cream.' Lance said. 'My favourite.'

The sleepout was made up for Bluey and Hakim had the guest room.

'Anyone for a nightcap?' Lance gravitated to the 1960's drinks cabinet with dimpled glass sliding doors and spindly legs.

'Just the one.' Blue plopped down on the settee and Hakim sat next to him.

'I'll have a Bailey's Irish Cream luv.' Gwen sat down in her chair and picked up her knitting.

'So, Abdul, you got family?'

Hakim nodded. 'I have in Iran a family.' He took a rum from Lance and sniffed the contents.

'It's rum mate. Bloody good shit.' Lance showed him the Bundy label. It went down like mother's milk.

'Blue?'

'Yeah mate.' Bluey took the rum and savoured the drink as it slid down.

'You got any sisters?'

'Sisters?'

'Ya know like brothers and sisters. Me and Blue. Same mum.'

'Ah. Yes I have two.' Hakim held out his glass as Lance offered a refill.

'Not married are ya?' Gwen asked. She pointed to the gold band on her finger. 'Lance and me, we're married,' she pointed to Lance. 'We have kids. Two. Rayleen and Darren.'

'No.' Hakim shook his head.

'He's a poof Gwen. Remember?'

'Oh, yeah. But they can get hitched.'

'Not in his country I bet. I bet they'd knock his bloody block off if he tried any of that malarkey.' Blue looked at Hakim.

'Go on. Ask him.'

Gwen took a deep breath to begin when Hakim took the smart phone and found google translate. He typed away and then showed the phone to Gwen.

I have two sisters and one brother. I am the oldest. My mother and father want to come to Australia.

'This is bloody brilliant.' Gwen read the translation. She typed,

Are you a poof? Can poofs get married in Iran. She showed the text to Blue.

'G'on then. Show him.' Gwen handed over the phone.

What is a poof?

It is a homosexual. Gwen handed the phone back.

Hakim read the words and looked at Bluey.

Blue is homosexual. I am not. I do not want to marry Blue.

Gwen read the text. She looked at Hakim and then at Bluey.

'Blue, you a'right.'

'Yeah.'

'Abdul thinks you're a poof.'

'What?'

'He reckons you're a poof and ya wanna get hitched.'

At this pronouncement Lance nearly choked on his drink. He cackled which turned into a belly laugh. 'That's the best thing I've heard all year. Blue is a poof and he wants to get hitched.' Lance wiped the tears from his eyes as he tried to stop laughing.

'Ya better tell him I'm not a poof Gwen. Type it, real fast.'

Gwen typed. 'He's not a poof either.'

'Whatdayamean?'

'He said he's not a poof at all.' Gwen smiled at Hakim and held out her glass for a top up.

'But he said he was gay.'

'I am gay.' Hakim smiled and chuckled in a jolly way. 'All the time gay.'

Gwen saw it straight away. Lance caught on about a second later and went into another fit of giggles. Blue felt vindicated.

'See. He's bloody gay.'

'He means, ya big galoot, that he's happy. Always happy.'

'Happy?' Blue had a hard time digesting the news.

'Yeah ya drongo. Happy.' Lance said and erupted in laughter once more. 'Ya killin' me Blue.' He held his stomach as it cramped.

Gwen texted the whole story and as Hakim read the translation he cracked a smile. The smile turned into a guffaw and then he set Lance off again, so much so that he had to leave the room or he'd die.

'And ya think ya going to New Bloody Zealand and ya end up here.' Lance sat back down with the bottle.

'New Bloody Zealand.' Hakim rolled his eyes and laughed.

'I pay a man. He say New Bloody Zealand. He is a bad man.'

'Too right. Bloody disgrace. Takin' money from a bloke like you and then dropping ya off God knows where.' Lance said.

'It's a shocker a'right.' Gwen held her glass for another Bailey's. Hakim did the honours. 'Ta.' Gwen resumed her knit one, purl one.

'And ya found ya way here. Among friends eh.' Lance poured another rum and handed the bottle around.

Blue took another rum, 'bloody lucky I reckon. I could'a missed him and he'd still be standin' there.'

'Bloody lucky I reckon.' Gwen nodded.

'I am lucky.'

'Too right.' Lance took the bottle and poured.

'So, whatcha gonna do now Abdul?' Gwen held her glass for another drink.

Hakim shrugged. 'I get a job. I bring my family.'

'That's the way.' Lance was all for getting a job. He had had one or two in his adult life. It wasn't his ideal, but Gwen insisted. Now he worked for the council, reading water meters. They gave him a very nice hat, and his bicycle was new.

'Now ya just can't go an' get a job. Just like that. Ya need things.'

'What sorta things?' Bluey was beginning to slouch on the settee.

'Blue. He need stuff. Refugee stuff. You're a refugee Abdul. Isn't that right?' Gwen smiled.

'I am Hakim.'

'What?'

'I am Adb al Hakim.' Hakim stood up. 'I am from Iran.'

'Yeah, got that.' Bluey sipped his rum.

'Anyroads, you got have all the stuff.' Gwen put her knitting down and took up her Baileys.

'I have.' Hakim found his suitcase and pulled out an identity card. He handed it over to Gwen.

'That's nice luv, but I reckon ya gonna need more than this.'

'Family.' Hakim showed his friends a picture of his family.

'She's pretty eh?'

'Nice.' Blue said.

'Rippa.' Lance looked at the worn photo.

Gwen stood up and rummaged around in the sideboard.

'Look at this.' She produced a picture of Bluey when he was about six years old. He was in shorts and a shirt, his hair parted in the middle and plastered down.

'That's that big bloke there.' She pointed to Bluey who had slumped to near supine on the settee.

112

'Gis a look Gwen.' Blue took the picture. 'I remember that.'

And then the albums came out. Gwen was the keeper of the family trust. She had all their history and they went through the ages and stages.

Rayleen and Darren were there, ad nauseum.

'Here's Ray in her dancing costume. Here's Darren in his scout uniform. Here's the kids on their bikes, with front teeth, without front teeth, with braces, without braces and it went on and on and on.

'Remember this?' Lance picked a picture and handed it to Gwen hoping to break the spell.

'Ya bloody had hair then luv.' Gwen showed the photo to Blue who started to laugh. Hakim began to giggle and soon everything was uproariously funny. Rum will do it to you every time.

Blue with no front teeth … hilarious.

Gwen with a beehive hairdo … side splitting.

Lance with hair … Blue nearly choked.

And then the killer. A picture of Lance at the races, his combover waving to the crowd like it was enjoying itself regardless of its owner.

Hakim rolled on the floor and grabbed his stomach. Blue wiped the tears from his eyes, but every time he looked at Lance he was off again. Gwen was cackling. But Lance? Lance was stony faced. He didn't see the joke and had gone stone cold sober. Rum will do that to you sometimes.

Rum is a cruel drink. It quickly sorts the men from the boys. It's propensity for a hangover is the stuff of legends. Bluey woke up with a crick in his neck from sleeping half on and half off the settee. He tried to feel his tongue but it was covered in something resembling the inside of an Ugg boot. He opened his eyes and closed them again. If he could just crawl to the bathroom, then he felt sure he would be able to face the day.

Hakim rolled onto his back and looked at the ceiling. He had no idea where he was or how he got there. The lightshade was a shade of purple he'd never seen before and the wallpaper made him seasick. He held onto the bed until the boat stopped rocking. If only he could get to the bathroom and try to throw up, he felt sure he'd be able to take a turn around the deck.

Lance groaned as Gwen got out of bed.
'I'll bring ya a nice cup of tea.' She put her dressing gown on and shuffled to the kitchen. Two rum bottles and an uncapped Baileys stood on the sink. There was an attempt to make some sandwiches which didn't come off, a box of half eaten chocolates, the wrappers strewn over the bench top and Lance's front plate with three false teeth soaking in a glass of rum.

Gwen popped a choccie in her mouth and tidied up the remnants of the party while the kettle boiled.

'Bloody gay.' She giggled.

She made up three trays for the invalids.

'Hakim?' Gwen tapped on the door of the guest room.

'Yes.' Hakim tried to focus on one spot.

'Can I come in?'

'Come in.'

Gwen opened the door and put the tray of the bed. The morning sun was streaming into the room and it was already getting hot.

'Just get this down and ya'll feel a lot better.' Hakim looked at the scrambled eggs and toast with a strong cup of tea. The eggs wobbled. Hakim's chin wobbled. He swallowed some tea and felt his stomach give a prayer of thanks.

'Thank you very much.'

'That's a'right luv.'

'Bluey?'

'Yeah.'

'I'm coming in.' Gwen put his eggs and tea down on the folding card table and opened the window.

'Thanks Gwen.' Blue looked at the breakfast and reached for the tea.

'I wanna talk to you when you spruce up a bit.'

'A'right.' Blue sat up and reached for his eggs.

Lance sat up and drank his tea while Gwen sat on the edge of the bed.

'Ya know he's got no-one and nowhere to stay.'

'Yeah.'

'Well I reckon he can stay here. Ya know, until he gets fixed up.'

'Yeah.'

'He could do some things around the house. We could get the papers and all the stuff he needs.'

'Yeah.'

'And let's face it Lance. We're the only family he's got in Straya.'

'Yeah.'

Gwen knew she was on a winner. After 40 years of marriage she knew Lance couldn't put two words together until at least 10 o'clock, and after a sesh like the night before it could stretch to midday.

Gwen, being a living dynamo, nipped down to the Salvos, on the hunt for a decent set of pants for Hakim. The Salvation Army second hand store was chock full of clothes. Some might have worked in the fashion stakes if you were a colour-blind American tourist. Why they insist on putting yellow and purple in a plaid is anyone's guess. Some of the clothes were obviously mistakes on the part of the purchaser in 1965, but Gwen had a good eye and could winnow the wheat from the chaff.

She came away with a bag of clothes and some very helpful information.

As the thermometer climbed on another scorcher of a day the men roused themselves to standing position and then began to walk.

Gwen came into the lounge room to see the three sitting in silence watching the tele. 'Three miracles in one day.'

She stood in front of the tele to grab their collective attention.

'Now listen. I bin thinkin' and here's the plan.' The men gave her their full attention.

'Hakim is stayin' here.' She smiled at Hakim and gave him a bag of clothes.

116

'Bluey, you gotta go back to work I'm thinkin'.'

'Yeah.'

'So after mum's op today ya can see her and then go tomorra.'

'A'right.'

'Lance luv, we gotta drive down to the council. They got papers we gotta sign so Hakim can live 'ere. I found all about it at the Salvos. They give ya a paper. Ya fill it in and sign and then he can stay. We gotta say we will look after him and he's not gonna get in any trouble or anythin'.'

'Hakim. Ya not gonna get in any trouble or anythin', are ya?'

'No trouble.' Hakim refrained from shaking his head.'

'So that's it,' she said, then added, an' I fed Ralph. For once he smells almost human.

'Thanks.' Blue smiled at his sister.

Gwen moved away from the tele. 'Now who wants a cuppa.'

All three sat up and begged.

'See, I told ya she'd know what to do.' Blue said.

Agnes's op was scheduled for 10 o'clock, then put back to 11, then 1pm. By the time Gwen and the gang arrived for the post op rundown Agnes was starving, mad as a cut snake because she'd miss Days of our lives, and fumin' at the free health system.

'Oh well,' Gwen said as she sat in the stupidly low chair next to the bed, at least you got to see ya mornin' show. Rise and Shine is it?'

'I've moved over to G'morning. R & Shine was getting boring.' Agnes was a discerning viewer.

'So when's ya op now Agnes?' Lance had found he could talk.

'3pm.' Agnes ground her teeth.

'I could tape it for ya mum,' Lance said. He was about the only person living on the planet who still had a working VHS tape machine. He'd never bothered to unplug it once his neighbour's son set it up. He'd only just mastered the remote control … some things are a necessity whether you like it or not.

'Can ya do that Lance?' Agnes's mood softened.

'Sure.' Lance gave his hair the once over, (over being the operative word) and puffed out his chest.

'Well ya better get crackin'. Agnes looked at the clock on the tele. Lance had 40 minutes to get home and the clock was ticking.

'A'right.'

'She looked well enough.' Gwen said as they walked to the car.

'Couldn't find a bloody bit of shade anywhere.' The car was melting in the sun. Ripples of heat shimmered over the bonnet.

Hakim grabbed the door handle,'Ouooou.'

'Bit hot eh?' Lance asked.

Hakim looked at his burnt fingers.

'Wait 'till ya get inside. It's enough to take ya breath away.' Lance opened the door and the hot air was like a fan forced oven.

The four adults sat in the car and began to sweat. Hakim put his seat belt on and the buckle seared his thigh. Blue kinda hovered over the seat hanging onto Gwen's headrest. His shorts offered little protection from the plastic overlay. Lance had never bothered to take it off; he figured he didn't use the back seat so it wasn't a problem.

Then, as with all hospital car parks some idiot was cruising around trying to find a park and holding up the traffic. Lance couldn't get out.

'Beep ya horn.'

'Nah, she'll be right.' They all waited as the temperature rose. You need to know that only one window worked. The driver side of course. Lance meant to get the others fixed, but he figured he didn't use 'em so why bother.

'Beep ya horn luv,' Gwen wiped the sweat from her face.

'Nah, all good.'

I should point out that Lance never used the horn for the simple reason it didn't work. He never used it so why bother. It had become his motto in life.

Hakim and Blue were looking like they were nearly ready to come out of the oven when the car blocking the artery moved on. Lance took the opportunity and backed out into the stream only to get stuck behind someone who was waiting for someone else to back out.

'Bloody hell.' Lance began to sweat. He began to wonder if he would get home in time for Days of our Lives. Agnes might never speak to him again if he missed it. (then again, there might be an upside!) Gwen might never speak to him again. He loved his wife -

'Get ya piece of junk moving or I'll move it for ya.' Lance yelled at the driver and it seemed to have the desired effect. The traffic thinned and Lance gunned the old Holden all the way home. He almost ran into the house and got down on his knees to press the required buttons and turned the tele on.

'Made it.' He sat on the floor and wondered how he was going to get up. Why the makers of television cabinets decided that we need to lie on our stomachs to press the on button is one of life's mysteries. The inventor of the remote control probably needs the Nobel Prize. The idea probably came to him at the chiropractors.

'I'll put the kettle on,' Gwen strode to the kitchen as Hakim and Blue plopped down on the settee and looked longingly at the air conditioner which didn't work. Lance once had the bright idea of cleaning the vents and filters. The task required a skill set that Lance sadly lacked. That, and he didn't have a screw driver to jerry rig it back together when he broke the little vital plastic lugs – all four and couldn't get it back in one piece.

It mocked the men sitting on the settee.

'Gis a hand willya?' Lance was on all fours trying to get up.

Hakim noted the man's dilemma. He roused himself to the job and offered a hand.

'Ta.' Lance pulled and that was that. His back chucked in the towel and the scream that issued from Lance could be heard down the block.

'What the …?' Gwen came rushing into the lounge room to see Lance on his knees, hanging onto Hakims hips, his face buried in Hakim's upper thigh.

'I. Can't. Bloody. Move.' Lance let out a yell.

It wasn't funny. It didn't have any of the hallmarks of a joke, but you know how it is. Someone is in pain and you just can't help yourself.

Blue let out a little giggle. Just a small one and offered advice. 'P'raps you could get back down to the floor?' He chuckled.

Lance tried backing out of the delicate situation.

'Yeeeeeeeeeeeeeeeiiiiiiiikkkkkkeeeeesss.' Blue stifled a laugh.

'P'raps you could just let him down on his face?' Gwen suggested.

'GGGwwwwwwwwaaaaaaaaarrrrrrrd.'

Hakim and Blue looked at one another and screwed up their faces to stop a guffaw. Bluey closed his eyes.

'You let go now.' Hakim felt the situation was getting drastic. He didn't want to spend his days looking like a porn star in a B rated movie. He grabbed Lance's hands from his buttocks.

'Hang on.' Blue grabbed Lance's legs.

'On the count of three.' Gwen wiped a tea-towel over her husband's brow.

'One, two, and they pulled Lance like he had a starring role in the inquisition.

'God Almighty.' Lance fell to the floor and his hair lay on the carpet imitating something the cat threw up. Well, that was the final straw. Blue laughed until he got a stitch, which set Hakim off and he wiped the tears with his sleeve which set Gwen to cackling. Lance? He lay on the floor and tried to figure out how the injury could be work related and how much worker's compo might be worth. There is an upside to every situation, he thought as Days of our Lives rolled to credits.

When the dust had settled Gwen suggested a BBQ for tea.

'It's ya last night. Hakim will be stayin' and well, I reckon he should have a real Ozzie BBQ. Sort of like a BBQ if ya know what I mean.'

'Rippa.' Blue knew a thing or two about his sister's legendary BBQs.

'We'll invite the neighbours. Rayleen and the kids, Darren and his intended.'

'He eats meat?' Gwen asked Blue.

'Bloody oath.' Blue would have said Hakim ate dirt if his sister was cooking it.

'Righty'o.' Gwen said and the small woman with a heart of gold, that stick of dynamite, that human dynamo got crackin'.

And Lance? He was deposited on the Lazyboy, a wizardry of a folding chair/bed with plastic webbing that is designed to catch your finger at least once in your lifetime, and acted in a supervisory capacity.

Blue and Hakim went shopping.

Blue looked at the list his sister had put in his hand with $100 dollars.

'See what ya can do Blue?' She had set the men a challenge. They didn't know how many mouths were to be fed. They hadn't a clue on what tabouli actually was and balsamic vinegar was so far off their radar it might have come from the moon.

He read the list until he recognised something he could understand.

'Prawns.'

'Prawns?'

'Yeah.' Blue could taste the cockroach of the sea smothered in garlic butter and dripping on his paper plate.

He drove up to the shopping centre and parked in the shade of a peppercorn tree.

'C'on.'

Hakim was wearing his own clothes, freshly laundered. I told you Gwen was a little dynamo.

'Ya know. I'm gonna get some stubbies and stuff.'

'Stubbies?'

'Yeah,' Blue led the way to a men's shop and pointed to the rows of shorts on the bargain table.

'Bloody wog.' A man slung the insult as he walked past Hakim.

'What?' Blue spun around and eyed the shopper. 'You got somethin' to say mate?'

'Wog.' The man nodded his head to Hakim.

'He's me mate. Watch it.' Blue stepped up to the mark. 'He's bloody from bloody I-ran. Pull ya head in ya don't know what ya talking 'bout.'

The shopper slunk away. 'Bat shit crazy.' Blue said to Hakim.

'Bat shit crazy.'

'Yeah.'

After a good twenty minutes trying to decide if the one colour on offer was suitable, Bluey bought three new pairs of stubbies, the Australian shorts that are the epitome of easy wear. No zips, no buttons, no fly. Just elastic that has the capacity to stretch in all directions. Under a beer gut, over a beer gut, around a beer gut. Stubbies are almost iconic … or … icono-lastic if you were a bit smarter than the average bear.

'Why don't cha get some?' He held up a pair for Hakim. Hakim shook his head. 'Strides then?' Blue picked a pair of King-gee working trousers. 'Beaut pockets.' Hakim shook his head.

'My shout.' Blue smiled.

'SHOUT.'

'Yeah.'

The assistant sidled up to Hakim.

'Can I help?'

'Nah, she's right.' Blue tried to figure Hakim's size.

'He's a 36 I reckon.' The woman took a good long look at Hakim. 'He's a very nice 36 if you ask me.' She picked out a pair of pants and handed them to Hakim.

'They went into the changing cubicles and came out looking like a pair of apprentice tradies who still lived at home.

'Told you he was 36. He's perfect.' She blushed. 'I mean, he's a perfect fit.'

'Yeah.' Blue looked at his stubbies. 'Only just managed to get the tackle in the box.

'Not you. Him.' The assistant looked at Hakim and her eyes took on a sparkle she reserved for men in the top ten category of her rather strict desirability list.

'Rippa.'

'Rippa mate.' Hakim smiled.

The supermarket manager helped them with the tricky ingredients on their list. She smiled at Hakim and if Blue knew anything about women, he reckoned she was flirtin'.'

'I think she likes ya.' Blue nudged Hakim as the woman bent down to pick pickled gherkins. She stood up and swept her hair over her shoulder and handed the gherkins to Hakim.

'Thank you very much.' Hakim gave his winning smile and then took the manager's hand and kissed it.

'Steady mate.' Blue grinned as the woman swooned.

'We need prawns luv.'

'Oh.' She drew an arabesque with her sensible shoe and blushed.

'Prawns?'

'We are BBQ.' Hakim let go of her hand.

She led the way when she was summoned by the loud speaker.

'Later.' She swept out of their aisle and was gone.

'Ya got 'em linin' up two abreast.' Blue slapped Hakim on the back.

It was as they passed the display of aboriginal art that Blue suddenly remembered Nellie's list. He found it in his wallet and read the contents. Naturally there was a tennis racquet, a set of books about horses and a scooter, number 9. There was also a Mega-jumbo-super-monster pack of Smith's crisps, a frypan, non stick, 8 pairs of thongs in various sizes and colours and a blow-up bed. Blue and Hakim had two trolleys by the time they had all they needed.

'I'll just chuck in a few of these colouring-in books and pencils. The kids love 'em.' Blue loaded the trolley up.

On the way out they passed a pet shop. Hakim cooed over the puppies and kittens in the window.

'This is beaut.'

'Yeah.' Blue went in the shop and patted the small mottled cattle dog in the display cage.

'It is beaut.' Hakim picked the pup up and it licked his face.

'Nothin' like a dog for company. Ralph and me go way back. I wouldn't be without him. He's me mate.'

'Mate.' Hakim rubbed the pup's tummy.

Blue cast his eye over the shop. They had everything for anything that walked, squawked, hopped, swam and dug. He came up to the counter with a bed for Ralph, a new collar, some pig's ear chews and those dentine chews that are supposed to keep your best friends mouth odour free.

'Ralph?' Hakim looked at the bundle on the counter.

'Yeah,' Bluey looked a bit sheepish, which was the only thing they didn't have in the shop. There is a line, somewhat fine, on the scale of pet it or eat it.

The shopping expedition's booty was thrown into the back of the ute and Blue put his swag over the lot.

'That's it then.' He looked at his sister's list.

'Bugger, we forgot the steak.'

'Steak.'

'Yeah.'

The Butchers was one of those old family businesses. Howard and Sons had been trading since Adam was a boy and knew a thing or two about meat.

Bluey and Hakim walked in and stood in line. The women were discerning customers.

'Not that one, this one next to the fatty one,' a woman jabbed at the glass display case.

'The skinny sausages, the kind without the skin,' a lady began to describe her 6 inch sausages and how she needed to constantly pull back the skin when they were cooking.

Blue and Hakim waited looking at the meat. He knew what his sister wanted. He had the list in front of him. He could read as well as the next man – except Hakim, who had trouble with English. But when his turn came Blue was at a loss.

What'llitbe?' Mr Howard asked.

Blue fell to bits in indecision.

'Well?'

'BBQ,' Hakim said.

'The BBQ pack?'

'Yes please.' Hakim nodded as the butcher began to pile meat on a poly tray. Sausages, lamb chops, steak, mince, spare ribs.

'Ya wanna bit o' bacon?'

'Um.' Blue watched as the meat resembled an abattoir.

'Lookin' for a bit of …'

'NO.' Bluey thought they should stop before he had to sell the car to pay for the stuff.

126

'Righty -o.' The Butcher weighed it up and totalled the price.

'It'll be worth it.' Bluey and Hakim put the meat in the ute. Gwen's a whizz with a BBQ.

Of course, an Aussie BBQ has time honoured rules.

Bluey and Hakim pulled out the folding chairs, set the plank of wood between two saw horses and chucked a truck load of ice in a kiddies blow up pool. Everything was going swimmingly.

The first to arrive was Rayleen and family. Her husband Rod let the kids, 5 and 7 loose in the back yard and they monopolised Ralph. Rayleen gravitated to the kitchen.

Next the neighbours arrived. Stavros and Thespona came with enough food for an extended tour of the Greek Isles. They had everything and then some. Gradually the back yard was populated with men, the women were in the kitchen, which is the natural order of things.

Bluey took centre stage as he ran over the details of how Hakim happened to be in Australia drinking beer and standing in a kiddies wading pool. It was a long story full of derring-do, life threatening moments and he had the crowd on the edge of their seats, or they might have been sitting on the cracked plastic seat which is like a pincer designed to grab what is usually reserved for the proctologist.

There were a lot of 'Never!, Jeez! Crickey and 'Ya shittin' me! and the old chestnut, New Bloody Zealand.' By the time Blue had saved Hakim's life a dozen times someone suggested they start the BBQ.

It's a man thing.

These days a piezo click and it's all over. But with a BBQ made from a 44 gallon drum and an iron hot plate all held in place with cross bars from nogging, it's a test to sort the men from the boys.

The men gravitated to the ring of fire. There was a discussion on the merits of firelighters versus a bit of kero. The kero won.

There was the debate on wood and hot coals versus kero and hot coals. The latter was chosen.

The only thing left was who was going to do the honours.

Hakim was appointed, after all it was his 'do.'

The kerosene was liberally squirted over the coals. Someone chucked in some newspaper and the matches were ceremoniously handed to Hakim.

'Let 'er rip mate.'

'Mate.'

Hakim struck a match.

They said the explosion could be heard a good 4 kilometres away.

What had presented itself as kero was in fact lighter fuel of a velocity that would take your hair off. Which is exactly what it did to Lance. Luckily his granddaughter Skyla had a mobile phone handy and snapped Grandpa as his hair went into shock.

Hakim was blown clean off his feet and landed in the wading pool, which was quite lucky really the fireman said, as he was on fire at the time.

Bluey was blown down the back still holding his beer and landed in a pile of grass clipping. Most of the men were in a state of shock.

What they all agreed upon was it was the best BBQ they had ever been to. Gwen and the girls outdid themselves.

The emergency services and the police stayed for a snag or two, someone brought music and Stavros wheeled over his Mega-Super BBQ with all the bells and whistles. It had a piezo lighter.

'I am lucky.' Hakim smiled at his new friends.'
'Bloody lucky mate.'

'You're one lucky bastard.'

'Rippa.' Hakim had arrived.

The morning after the night before is always a bit of a let-down. Seeing the back yard in a state of disrepair Lance shrugged and took the line of least resistance.

'Ah well. Now we can do a complete reno.' Of course we all know Lance well enough to suggest it's never gonna happen.

But what took your eye from the fire, the deflated pool, the burnt-out 44-gallon drum and the mountain of beer cans was the white fluff adorning the grass.

'What is it?' Lance said from his chair. Blue scratched the back of his neck for a second and then it dawned.

'I dunno?' He hunted for Ralph who was nowhere to be seen.

'It's fluff or somethin'.' Gwen said.

'I just dunno.' Blue walked over the yard and looked for his dog.

Ralph had been having fun. His new collar was chewed to a red pulp. His bed, which had been lovingly prepared by the grandkids was strewn all over the yard, in bits about as big as an orange. But to top off the whole scene Ralph had been busy… digging. The backyard looked like the Somme.

Bluey whistled up his best mate.

Ralph jumped the fence and bounded up to his master. He was frisky, full of life. He was also full of sausages.

He farted.

'Good lord,' Gwen pulled her apron over her nose and retreated inside.

'Jeez, that pan licker could strip paint,' Lance, despite his worker's comp back, shot inside and closed the door.

'And I gotta travel 10 hours with you.'

Ralph jumped up and tried to lick Bluey's face.

Git.

Ralph Git.

Bluey was having his last cup of tea and a few left-overs sitting at the kitchen table with Hakim, when there was a knock at the door. They continued with cold lamb chops and potato salad listening to the conversation at the front door.

'Dept of …. Interview…..Ms Rentree…..Hakim.'

'Look lively, I think ya got a visitor.' Blue poked Hakim in the ribs with his elbow.

Gwen ushered the Government Case worker into the kitchen and offered her a chair.

'Just sit luv an' I'll put the kettle on.'

The men looked at the Government official.

Sylvia Rentree was one of those women who looked like she took no nonsense. She had purple hair, a nose ring, an attitude that made her narrow her eyes at anything resembling a moderate voter and a forefinger that was used for poking any moderate voters in the chest.

'I'm Ms Sylvia Rentree.' She stuck out her hand and offered it to Hakim.

He stood up and took the hand, and was about to pull out all the stops vis-à-vis flirting when Bluey gave him a look that a mother might give a three year old when they about to commit a heinous crime.

Don't do it!

Hakim took the hint.

'I am very pleased to meet you.' He let go of Medusa's hand and sat down.

'She's from the Government Hakim.' Gwen set out the teapot and mugs.

'Government.'

'That's right Mr Hakim.' Ms Rentree said. 'We are here to process you. She used the royal '*we*' because in social interaction 101 they taught that to get a handle on the situation you need to show you have a vast team behind every decision. Sylvia's vast team was a supervisor, a girl who did the filing and the tea lady. Money was tight in the public service.

'Process?'

'Yes. We need all your particulars, all your background, your intentions, your future aims and your bank balance.'

'I have.' Hakim fetched his ID card and handed it over.

Sylvia ran her fingers through her hair and jangled her bangles.

'This is …'

'It's all he's got luv.' Gwen poured the tea.

'Well how did he get here?'

'Well,' It was all Bluey needed in the way of encouragement. Lance shuffled into the kitchen and sat down, poured himself a cup of tea and opened a packet of biscuits.

'Ya gonna love this.' He sat back and waited to be entertained. A good yarn is worth listening to twice, or three times in Lance's case.

Naturally as a yarn gets its momentum and is refined in the telling, it gets somewhat bigger, more dangerous, hilarious in parts and pathos is always a good cliff-hanger. Bluey was in that expansive mood … again. He took a deep breath and began and didn't stop until he had brought it all up to date.

'So that's about it.' Blue felt he had acquitted himself with flying colours.

Ms Rentree sat, stony faced, throughout.

'I am taxi driver.' Hakim gave his winning smile. It didn't cut the mustard with Sylvia. She was one of those women who wasn't swayed easily when it came to flattery. She was more interested in the injustices of the world, especially injustices to women, especially injustices to women when it was the man's fault … and according to Sylvia it was always the man's fault. Why she was in the Department of Social Services attached to the Department of Immigration which was under the auspice of someone in Canberra – probably eating Monte Carlo biscuits at their desk, was anyone's guess. Sylvia wanted to be on the front-line fighting injustices, but paying the bills was one of life's necessities.

'So Mr Hakim,' Sylvia tapped her officious pen on the mountain of forms laid out on the kitchen table, 'shall we begin?'

Lance glanced at Gwen and raised his eyebrows. Gwen nodded knowing just what her husband meant. This Ms Rentree was a hard nut to crack.

'Biscuit luv?' Gwen offered her homemade delights.

'No, thanks.' Ms Rentree looked at Gwen fussing in the kitchen, a slave to domesticity. She narrowed her eyes.

'Ms Cracknell?'

'Yes luv?'

'You're not a slave you know.'

'Pardon?' Gwen looked over to the table with the sink chain in her hand.

'You have a life of your own,' Sylvia said looking at Lance and Bluey. She reserved a withering stare for Hakim. After all, she surmised, he came from a society that typically kept women barefoot and pregnant.

'Of my own?' It was news to Gwen.

'Don't you want a life of your own Ms Cracknell?'

'I have all the life I can handle right now luv. What with me mum, Lance, Rayleen and the kids, Darren and his intended and now Hakim.'

'Yes, but what about what *you* want?' Sylvia began to get on her high horse and the air up there was rarefied.

'Me?' It came out a small squeak.

'Yes, you. Free yourself from the shackles of the kitchen. Branch out.'

'You mean burn me bra, or something?' Gwen said. Lance gave her a small lecherous leer.

'Bigger,' Sylvia said.

'Like put me feet up and watch the tele?'

'Bigger.'

'Like, I dunno, go to one of them spa places for a weekend or something. On me own.' Gwen looked at Lance. He began to feel sick. 'Gwen, luv.'

Gwen smirked at her husband. 'Just a thought luv, just a thought.'

- and we all know what thought did-

'Ms Cracknell,' Sylvia began when Bluey stepped up to the mark,

'Sorry to interrupt and everything, but I gotta get crackin' and will this take long. I got a long drive.'

The word mansplaining cropped up in the tirade of male domination, male supremacy and male egocentric world, but it all went over Bluey's head as he was thinking on the road ahead.

Hakim looked at Bluey.

'Get crackin' mate.'

'Yeah.' Bluey nodded.

Sylvia readjusted her offence -o-meter and shuffled her papers.

'Thanks sis.' Bluey stood up. Hakim stood up. There was an awkward moment when they stood about not sure if it was acceptable to hug.

Hakim slapped Blue on the shoulder. Blue gave Hakim a punch on the forearm.

'Mate.'

'Mate.'

It said more than a hallmark card.

The mob trooped out to the front fence and watched Blue take off down the road in first gear with Ralph hanging out of the window. It was rush hour in the suburbs. He nearly saw a car on the corner and the brake lights flickered and then he was gone.

'If we could just get the process underway,' Sylvia walked back inside and picked up her pen.

She opened up the pack supplied from the office. The title was optimistically upbeat.

REGISTRATION, ASSIMILATION,
NATURALIZATION

'Now, I have a list of questions I would like you to answer.' Sylvia said and looked at her watch.

Of course, there would be a bit of paperwork first. Nothing is that simple when the public service is involved, or the Government.

Immigration is just a word, but a big one with myriad of nuances.

Immigrant or refugee.

Nomadic or visitor.

Asylum seeker or wanted by the police – or both.

It was all in the detail.

Lance nodded off. Gwen took up her knitting and Hakim developed a headache.

'Now, Hakim,' Sylvia said as she glanced at her watch, 'what are your long-term goals in Australia?'

'She means what are you gonna do?' Lance woke up and put it in plain-splaining.

'I get dog.'

There are few things in life more satisfying than getting a dog. A dog is a mate like no other.

The pet shop in the shopping centre went overboard when someone wanted to buy a dog. There was the adoption certificate, the memento booklet for photographs and the like, the instructions on getting a Facebook page and a voucher for the first free shampoo.

Gwen, Rayleen and the two kids took Hakim to the shop. Once Rayleen had prised the kids off the kittens and guinea pigs the children helped Hakim pick his dog.

'Call her fluffy.' Skyla said.

'Call her Bob,' Bob said. He didn't have much imagination at 5 years old.

'Beaut.' Hakim said.

Hakim handed over some of his interim payment from the Government and Rayleen and Gwen chipped in for the collar, the bed, the bowl and a, soon to be, really annoying squeaking duck.

Beaut was a cattle dog with a bit of something thrown into the mix.

'A bitsa.' Lance said when he saw the pup.

'Bits-a this and bits-a that.'

'Beaut.' Hakim sat down in the Somme, aka back yard and fell in love.

A puppy is a full time occupation. So is being a refugee. Hakim was required to furnish the Australian Government with so much of his life history he felt like making it up, but keeping track of a lie is like keeping hold of a slippery eel.

Ms Rentree was, if not exactly a happy employee, resolutely wedded to her job. Rent will do that to a person. She had a few 'clients' as the public service like to call the public who had the misfortune to fall under their wheels of bureaucracy. The Somalian family were friendly, but the wife was one of the downtrodden minorities. The Italian husband and wife were nice, but Maria so needed to get out from under the yoke of male oppression. Mr Stravinska from Bosnia was charming, but had an attitude to women that needed severe adjustment.

She had yet to make a judgement on Hakim, but his standing in her eyes wasn't looking good. He came from somewhere that might be described as a regime. He came from a place where women were treated like women and he was too handsome to be a persecuted minority, in mortal danger or have a police record. He was just too darn nice!

But Ms Rentree had pencilled him in every day. She was determined to get to the bottom of the story.

It was on day three, when she was eating one of Gwen's macaroons and stirring her tea when it occurred to her she was missing a vital piece of information.

And then, for all Ms Rentree's dislike of anything that smacked of toxic sentimentality she asked the one question that so far had not been thought of.

'Why?'

'Why?' Hakim ran his fingers through his hair.

'Yes, Hakim. Why?'

Why would anyone leave their family, their home and pay money to a shonky people smuggler and travel half way around the world ... or a bit further if you thought you were going to New Bloody Zealand.

Gwen, Rayleen, Lance, Rod, Skyla and Bob all sat at the kitchen table waiting for an answer. Bob was especially interested because 'why' was his favourite word at the moment.

Hakim picked up Beaut and rubbed her ear. Ms Rentree sat with pen poised over paper.

'I am taxi driver.'

'Got that.' Gwen said.

Hakim looked at the family. He smiled at Sylvia who smiled back, then checked herself.

'I drive wrong man.'

Then, via google translate, hand signals and broken English the story emerged.

I don't want to take the thunder from Hakim, but I'll give you the good oil, it will be quicker in the long run.

Hakim was a taxi driver in Tehran. It was a Wednesday, not that the day of the week has much influence on the story, but this particular Wednesday he pulled his taxi up to the government building in the centre of the city and a neatly dressed official got in.

The destination was a tea house not far away. Tehran is a teaming metropolis of around 15 million give or take a few. You can't squeeze that many people into a small space and not have a traffic jam or two. Hakim pulled out all the stops to get to his destination in one piece and on time.

He arrived at the tea house and was given a sizable tip. His passenger got out and that was that. Except his important passenger left his briefcase on the seat. So being the conscientious person Hakim is, he hopped out of his taxi and ran after the official.

And that's when the photographer from the newspaper snapped his picture.

The front page the next day saw Hakim in conference with three Government detractors.

In Iran, you can be having tea with the Minister of Intelligence at ten o'clock and by three your face is on the most wanted list. It's a fast-paced political sphere and is something akin to standing on a greased bowling ball. It's hard to keep track of who's Instagram account you should follow, who not to name a sandwich after and who you should pick up in your taxi.

Mr X as he was known in the newspaper was purported to be a top, high level security risk.

In Iran you can be a taxi driver in the morning, to a high-level security risk called Mr X before lunch.

Hakim didn't wait to get a phone call when he saw his picture on the front page of the paper. Politics moves fast in Iran. Hakim moved faster!

'But couldn't you just explain?' Ms Rentree pleaded, caught up in the injustice of the story.

'No.' Hakim said.

'I'm not sure if it's true, but I read on Facebook that they cut your tongue out in Iran.' Rayleen said.

'Pretty hard to explain without ya tongue.' Lance said.

Bob poked his tongue out and his sister pretended to cut it off as Beaut jumped up and tried to lick it. The kids left the adults to it and took the dog outside.

'I read they cut ya bloody block off.' Rod drew his finger across his throat. Rayleen, his wife, gasped.

'No.'

Hakim nodded

'That's bloody bad luck luv?' Gwen said.

'Bad man. Bad luck.' Hakim fiddled with his mug of tea.

'Well, this changes everything. You are a political refugee.' Sylvia's eyes lit up. What a coup. Hakim wasn't your average refugee, asylum seeker or immigrant. She had a real live political refugee. Her standing in the office would jump a notch or two. She might even get a mention in dispatches to Canberra.

'Do ya think them James Bond types will come after him?' Lance asked.

Sylvia's eyes widened. Her mind wandered to the Nobel Peace Prize, movie rights, a book, the sky was the limit.

'Not on my watch.' Sylvia thumped the table with her fist and her bangles jangled.

'I guess if they do start looking for ya, they'll go to New Bloody Zealand.' Lance said.

They all had a bloody good laugh.

The life of a political refugee is a full and varied one. There are the things you need to do, the things you want to do and the things you must do. Hakim tried to juggle the various tasks while he waited for Sylvia Rentree to give him permission to do the things she wanted him to do, the things she needed him to do and the things she thought he must do. That none of these wants, needs and musts were the same only made the tasks more complicated. It was just your typical public service triplicate.

While Hakim waited he visited Agnes every day at the hospital and they'd watch the television together. The tele is a great way to learn a language, and the hospital was air conditioned, the food quite appetizing and the nurses accommodating.

'G'day.' Hakim said. Agnes took her eye off the tele long enough to watch him sit down.

'Just in time,' Agnes said and turned her attention to a re-run of *I love Lucy*.

At the first commercial she shared her news. 'Doc says I can go home tomorra. Tell Gwen will ya.'

'Tomorra?'

'Yeah.'

They watched Lucy for the next three minutes.

'I reckon about 3ish.' Agnes said.

'Three-ish.' Hakim nodded and passed some grapes to his companion.

'Doc said one of me bunch of grapes was a big as this one,' she popped a green grape in her mouth.

Hakim frowned. He was floundering with the nuance of the conversation.

'Ya know, me piles. We all got 'em ya know. The Gaylore's are known for 'em.' Agnes explained and mimed with the bunch of grapes. Hakim nodded and then they turned their attention to Lucy and Ethel.

He made it through *I love Lucy*, *I dream of Jeanie*, *The price is right* and *The young and the Restless* when the trolley came around for lunch.

'Ya stayin'?' Agnes asked.

'Nah.' Hakim said and shook his head. 'Interview.' The trolley woman put the extra plate away. Hakim had charmed her all week to such an extent that she was saving a jelly and custard every day, just in case he was coming.

'Well, tell Gwen will ya?'

'No worries mate.' Hakim said and smiled at the trolley woman. She passed him a packet of three biscuits on the way out.

The bus ride home was always pleasant. The bus could have taken a straight line in half the time, but it wends its way through the suburbs and the view to Hakim was a delight.

The Australian suburbs are vast, on the whole homogenous, and look like they could do with a good rain. The few people with green lawns put up signs saying bore water, so they don't get a fine from the council and rocks on their roof from envious neighbours or a letter of complaint.

Hakim sat at the front opposite the driver for a better view of the road.

'Bloody get outta the way ya drongo.' The driver wasn't the usual amicable man, but a 'nut job' as Hakim heard someone behind him explain.

'I hate my job.' The driver, whose nametag on his coat hanging on the back of his chair said, Doug.

'For fuck's sake.' Doug threw the bus around a parked car and the passengers hung on, tight.

'Watch it.' A man in the handicapped seat yelled as his shopping slid across the floor. Hakim rescued the rolling oranges.

'Thanks mate.'

'Mate.' Hakim smiled.

'Jeez, ya idiot.' Doug was having a bad day. He pulled up in a busy street about 50 metres from the bus stop and waited for his passengers.

They stood at the stop and looked at the bus.

'I'm surrounded by drongos.' Doug flung his little gate open and leaned out of the by-fold door.

'Hurry up ya morons.'

The group of customers began to trot to the bus.

'We were waiting back there,' a woman with a shopping trolley climbed aboard.

'Well ya can see I can't stop there, some idiot parked their car in the bloody bus stop didn't they.' Doug glared at the passengers in his interior mirror as they filed down. He closed his door when a young woman said,

'Wait up. There's one more.'

'He better hurry up.' Doug revved the engine. 'I haven't got all day ya know.'

'He's only got one leg,' the woman said. The passengers all looked to the window and watched the man slowly make his way to the bus.

Doug tapped his fingers on the steering wheel as he waited.

"bout bloody time.' Doug shut the doors and before the man could sit down he was off. Hakim grabbed the man and deposited him in a chair.

'Thanks mate.'

'Mate.'

'I hate my job.' Doug's day wasn't getting any better.

When Hakim arrived home, Ms Rentree was sitting in the kitchen eating a slice of sponge cake and drinking tea, discussing the various methods of removing stubborn stains.

'G'day.' Hakim walked in and sat down.

'G'day Hakim.' Gwen poured a cup of tea.

'I have news.' Hakim said. The women waited as Hakim's brain worked in English.

'Doc says I can go home tommorra, 'bout three ish.'

'That's me mum all over.' Gwen smiled at Hakim.

'Well I have news too.' Sylvia opened her folder and took out a form. She handed it over to Hakim with a flourish. He looked over the words and shook his head.

'It says,' Sylvia began, 'that you can start night school.'

'School?'

'Yes. To learn English.' Sylvia sat back and sipped her tea. Places at night school were hard to come by. She had practically begged funding for Hakim.

'It comes with a bus pass.' Sylvia waited for the shower of thanks, the accolades of excellence to rain upon her.

'School.' Hakim frowned. He felt out of his depth.

'Does he really need to go?' Gwen could see his discomfort.

'Absolutely.' Sylvia said. She couldn't see a problem.

'Listen luv, I don't want to tell you ya job or anything, but I reckon Hakim here should think about it for a bit. Ya know, just to get used to the idea.'

'But his lessons start tomorrow.' Sylvia said. 'It's for beginners.'

'I go.' Hakim bit his lip and managed a small smile for Sylvia. 'I am no drongo.'

'No luv, ya certainly not a drongo.' Gwen cut a second slice of cake for Ms Rentree.

It was only 24 hours and Ms Rentree's feet were ensconced under the kitchen table once again. She put an Anzac biscuit on her plate and pulled out a wad of forms.

'You'll never believe it Gwen.'

'What now? University?'

'I have found Hakim a job.' This fact was quite a feat. As yet Ms Rentree hadn't found any of her brood a job. The Somalian family had special needs in regards to their suitability for work. Mr Xaabsade didn't want to do any work that a woman could do. Mrs Xaabsade didn't want to do any work that might interact with men. It was a tight fit in the workplace. Maria and Anthony liked the idea of work, but with their extended family already in the suburbs, they were kept quite busy. Mr Stravinska was sure he was being followed by the Bosnian mafia and was a nervous wreck. He spent most of his day with the blinds drawn, watching the street.

'A job.'

'I know. Amazing isn't it.'

'Sure is.' Gwen set the mugs out, giving Sylvia her favourite green.

'Where is he?'

146

'Gone with Lance to get me mum.'

'Oh.'

'Should be back any tic.'

'Right.' Sylvia looked at her watch. Mr Stravinska could wait.

'Mum, this is Sylvia. Sylvia this is me mum, Agnes.' With the formalities out of the way Agnes plopped herself gingerly down on the settee and reached for the remote.

'I got the tape Agnes.' Lance looked at the tape near the floor.

'I get it.' Hakim had no trouble bending down to retrieve the recording.

'Put it on will ya luv. I know what happens, but I'll watch anyway.' Agnes was ensconced for the duration. Lance looked at his spot on the settee and resigned himself to the fact that he wouldn't get near it for at least a week, maybe two. Hakim fluffed up a cushion and fussed.

'Don't fuss luv, I'm a tough ol' bird.'

'No worries.'

'Hakim, Sylvia wants a word.' Gwen said from the kitchen doorway.

The Anzac biscuits were handed around and Sylvia tapped the wad of forms in front of her.

'I got you a job.' She smiled and nodded.

'Job?'

'Yes. Work.'

'What kinda job?' Lance had grand plans for Hakim. There was the electric windows in the car, the lawn to mow, the front door to fix, the sliding garage door. His plans were expansive.

'Well …' Sylvia waited for the ta-daa moment. 'He will be a TA to a handyman.'

'A TA?' Gwen asked.

'Trade assistant.'

'Navvy.' Lance said.

'Job?' Hakim couldn't quite believe it.

'Yes. And Mr West said he can start tomorrow. He'll pick him up at 6.'

'Job.' Hakim said. 'I am stunned mullet.'

Gwen thought it would be just the thing to get him on his feet. Lance hoped he could take the tools on the weekend and Sylvia considered Hakim her star pupil, a gift and that he was quite handsome didn't hinder her opinion at all.

'Bloody rippa.'

'You said it.' Lance decided it required a beer.

With the forms signed Sylvia left with a spring in her step.

'And don't forget your lesson tonight Hakim. 7 sharp.'

'Lesson?'

'School.' Gwen said.

'No worries.' He waved Sylvia away as little Beaut ran around in circles.

'I am having worries.' Hakim confided to Gwen.

'Nah, she'll be right luv. Just do ya best.'

Eugène Winnap Memorial school for girls gave their school classrooms over to the common good twice a week for a tidy sum of money.

Hakim stood about at the entrance gate and wished he was somewhere else. He was a taxi driver and didn't like school.

Several pupils of various ethnicities pushed past him and he took a deep breath and followed.

The classroom was spacious, well-it and had about half a dozen students already seated.

'I am new.' Hakim said to a man standing at the blackboard.

'Ah, name?'

'I am Adb al Hakim'

'Sit.' The teacher pointed to a desk.

The clock hit 7pm and the man closed the door.

Hakim swallowed hard and put his book and pencil on the desk.

'Good evening Ladies and Gentlemen My name is Mr Smallwood.' Don Smallwood wrote his name on the blackboard.

Hakim wrote it down.

'This is your first lesson in English.' Don wrote the number one on the blackboard.

'One becomes first.'

Hakim wrote it down. The rest of the class were staring in awe.

'Two becomes second.' The blackboard was filling up.

'Three becomes third.'

Turd.' A man at the front said and laughed. His joke was lost on the pupils as they grappled with the numbers. Mr Smallwood eyed the joker. There was always one.

'Now I will call your name. Please stand up and tell us where you come from.'

'Mr Peche.'

'Slovakia,' a large man said as he brushed breadcrumbs from his shirt front.

'Mr Van de Berg.'

The joker stood up. 'I am Dutch.' He turned to the class and bowed. ' Bak Van de Berg from Holland vith de vindmills.' Mr Van de Berg threw his arms into the explanation as the class sat open mouthed. Half probably didn't know where Holland was and the other half didn't know what a vindmill vas.

'Thank you Mr Van de Berg.' Mr Smallwood tried to restore order.

'Miss Gombombo.'

'Gambia,' a small woman chirped and quickly sat down.

'Adb al Hakim.'

'Iran.' Hakim looked at his fellow students. They nodded. He sat down.

There were people from all over the world. Morocco, Sudan, Russia, Indonesia, China and beyond. Mr Stravinska didn't make it. It was too risky after dark. Mr and Mrs Xaabsade couldn't get a baby sitter, but that didn't matter, Hakim felt he belonged to that rare and unified tribe, the new Australian.

Mr Don Smallwood was a seasoned teacher. He knew the perils and pitfalls of the new immigrant in grappling with English. It was best to assume his students knew nothing of verbs, syntax, sentence structure and pronunciation.

He smiled.

'We will start with a greeting. Repeat after me.'

'Good morning.'

'Good morning.' The class echoed.'

'This is said when we see someone before lunchtime or 12 midday.' Mr Smallwood drew a clock on the blackboard and divided it up into morning, afternoon and night. Hakim copied it down. And so, the lesson continued until an hour and a half later the teacher put his chalk down and his pupils breathed a little easier.

'Good bye.' Miss Gombombo said and rushed out the door.

'See ya.' Mr Van de Berg waved and strode out the door.

'Mr Peche nodded and left. He wasn't going to chance a goodbye when he might get it wrong.

Hakim smiled at his teacher. 'Good bye.'

'Wanna come for a drink mate?' Mr Van de Berg collared Hakim as he stepped out into the night.

'I have job.'

'Just a quickie eh?'

'I have job.'

The pub was crowded and the air conditioning was struggling to keep up. Bak looked at his new friend.

'What'llitbe?'

'Beer?' Hakim said, adding. 'SHOUT.'

'No worries mate.' Bak stood back and let Hakim struggle through the throng to the bar.

'Beer please, two.'

'Schooners or pots luv.' The barmaid asked.

'Beer please two.' Hakim put his money on the bar.
'Schooners it is.'

The pupils found a bench outside and sat down in the cool night air.
'So ya from I-ran eh?' Bak said.
'Iran.' Hakim nodded. 'You speak the good English.'
'Yeah, but I can't write it, an' I need to write for the job.'
'Oh.' Hakim smiled.
'I am not good.'
'Nah, bloody easy mate. Just pick up the lingo on the job.'
'Lingo?'
'The language.' Bak finished his beer.
'My shout eh? One for the road.'
The road was a long one. Three beers each and then last orders were given.
'See ya next week eh?'
'Yes. I am coming.'
'Wouldn't miss it for quids eh?'
'Pardon.'
'Never mind. You'll get the hang of it.' Bak slapped Hakim on the back and was gone.

On the bus ride home Hakim looked over his notes. He practiced his greetings to the bus driver.
'Good evening.'
'What's up mate?' The driver sniffed. 'No trouble mate. Sit down and shut it.'

At his stop he said,
'Thank you very much.' Have a pleasant evening.'
'Not a prob mate. See ya next time.' The driver shut the door and moved off.

Gwen was waiting for him.

'Good evening. I hope you had a pleasant evening?' Hakim said as he walked in the door.

'Not bad, ya-self?' Gwen said as she put the kettle on.

'Not bad.' Hakim reverted to easy speak.

Over tea and cake Gwen and Lance put Hakim straight on what he had gleaned from his first English lesson.

It's not good evening, but how's things.

Its not Good Morning, but 'mornin'.'

Its not Good bye and I hope to see you soon., but see ya round, mate.

Hakim practiced until he was word perfect.

'Now ya better get some shut eye. I'll get ya up in time for this fella that's comin' tomorra.'

'She means, if you'd like to retire to bed, she will awaken you in good time for your appointment with your employer.' Lance cacked himself.

'Git.'

Hakim git.

Mr West drove an old ute with everything strapped to it with string, wire, old ratchet straps and bicycle tubing. The ladder balanced precariously on the roof of the cab and was fastened with an old belt at the back. In amongst all the tools, the esky the drink cooler and an air compressor was a dog. Sparky was the laziest dog this side of the black stump.

Hakim was waiting out the front before 6 sitting on his esky, dressed in his King-gee trousers and his blue shirt.

'Saw ya sittin' there like a cocky on a fence.' Reginald West hung out of the driver's side window and pushed his towelling hat back on his head.

'Well ya comin' or what?'

'I am comin' Hakim gave Beaut a pat and stood up.

'That your mutt?'

'Pardon?'

'That your mate there.' Reg pointed to Beaut.

'Yes. My mate.'

'Bringin' it then?'

'She can come?'

'That's what I said. Now c'on.'

Hakim sat in the ute and felt right at home.

'Mornin'. I am Hakim.'

'Yeah, I'm Reg. That sheila with the coloured hair said you'd be wantin' a job. Ya good with ya hands eh?'

'Yes, I am good.'

'No worries then.' Reg put the old ute in gear and they were off.

'No worries mate.'

Reg West was in his late 50's and could fix anything for the right price. He was a plumber by trade, but that didn't stop him from putting up a fence, pulling down a shade house or installing an air-conditioner .

'We got ta put a bloody cat flap in this mornin'. Some ol' tart with a cat or someit.'

Hakim nodded. He had no idea what Reg had said.

The old tart was in the better part of town. Reg pulled up and looked at the house.

'Bloody nice pile of bricks?'

'Nice.'

'C'on then.'

Hakim was loaded up with tools and followed with the dogs at his heels.

The job entailed a hole to be cut, the flap to be fitted and the bill to be presented.

Reg looked at the cat flap the woman presented and scratched the back of his neck. He sucked in his breath and shook his head.

'Sorry luv, this'll never fit.' Reg was mulling over the problem of a panelled door and no flat space for a flap.

They all stood on the verandah looking at the door waiting for Reg to get some divine inspiration. Beaut and Sparkie sat in the shade panting.

'Well?' The woman was paying by the hour and wanted to know if standing around scratching your head would be included.

'The problem I see luv is that ya got the wrong flap or someit.'

Hakim looked at the woman and smiled.

'Well?'

'Well, it's like this. We could come back tomorra. You need a skinny flap or someit.' Reg shrugged his shoulders and rolled his eyes in the direction of Hakim.

Hakim looked at the problem. He smiled and said, 'I can do.'

Reg took a step back and looked at his assistant then took a phone call.

The job took an hour, the morning tea the woman provided another half hour which went on the bill.

'A man's gotta live ya know.' Reg said as he made up the paperwork.

The day progressed. They dug a hole, well when I say they, I mean Hakim. Reg had some paperwork to do and answered the phone. They installed a window. When I use plural, I mean Hakim as Reg needed to get some supplies from the hardware store and answer the phone. They fixed a pool filter; which Reg supplied the knowhow and Hakim the brute force while Reg answered the phone, and ended the day with a beer … or two.

'So, Hakim, whatchadoin' in Straya?' Reg lined up the beers and made himself comfortable.

'In Straya?'

'Yeah.'

'I am a political refugee.'

'Cripes.' Reg's eyes stood out like organ stops.

'I am from Iran.'

'I-ran eh.' Reg downed his beer.

'Wog.' The word was thrown down the bar and ended at Reg.

'Watch it mate. He's with me.' Reg stood up and pushed his hat back. 'You got a problem I'll sort ya out.'

The bar patrons resumed their drinking.

'Bloody ijits.' Reg said.

'Ijits?'

'Yeah, you said it.'

'SHOUT.' Hakim put his money on the bar.

'Mate, ya don't need to shout it.'

Hakim took his money off the bar.

'Nah, I mean ya don't need to SHOUT it.' Reg pulled the note from Hakim's hand and put it on the bar. 'Ya say, my shout.'

'My shout.'

'Yeah. Too right.'

Another two beers were lined up.

'Reg, what is wog?'

'Ah, don't ya be worryin' about that.' Reg sipped his beer.

'It's a foreign type.' The barmaid said. 'Someone who's not from here.' She wiped the bar and smiled at Hakim. He smiled back and she blushed.

'More than that,' The barman said, 'It's a bloke who's a bit on the sunburnt side.'

'Sunburnt?' Hakim frowned.

'Ya know, dark like. Sorta from them Arabie countries.'

'And the I-ties. They were always called wogs.' An old bloke chipped in.

'And the gyppos too.' A man drinking stout said, 'from Egypt.'

'And don't forget them from Greece.'

'Nah, mate they weren't wogs.'

'True?'

'Dinkum.'

'Am I wog?'

'Yeah. But ya a good wog. Sorta a reffo and they're different.'

'That's right.' The barmaid, Helen put the peanuts closer to Hakim.

'I am political refugee.'

'Jeez.' The patrons at the Centennial Arms felt this small snippet of information was worth savouring. Vicarious fame has its attractions.

'Were you in danger?' Helen asked forgetting the other drinkers.

'Too right.'

'Shot at?'

'Yeah.' Hakim couldn't help himself.

'Jeez.' Helen poured him a beer and forgot to ring it up.

Reg felt his standing at the bar increase with every revelation.

'I gave him a job ya know.'

'Mate.' The Barman slapped Reg on the back and gave him a beer. 'On the house.'

157

'Ta very much.'

'So ya come to Oztraalia to escape.'

'Yeah.' Hakim smiled at all his new friends. 'I was out bush and then came to the big smoke. Bloody lucky mate.'

The crowd nodded. 'A fella can hide in the big city,' the stout drinker said.

'So what's ya story mate?'

And Hakim began his yarn. You can't spend a few days with Bluey and not pick up a pointer or two when it comes to a good yarn.

Of course, there was the footy match, the snake, Plinthe Hill and after about half a dozen beers he finished with digging a hole.

A bloke from the other end of the bar piped up,

'Ya never went 'round Plinthe Hill.'

'Too right.'

A legend was born.

'See ya tomorra.' Reg drove away leaving Beaut and Hakim on the footpath. Beaut ran around in a circle for about thirty seconds then fell down, asleep. Hakim yawned and stretched. His back hurt, his hands hurt, but it felt good to be doing something worthwhile. He stood on the verandah and looked at the front yard and a thought took hold.

'Ya comin' in or what?' Agnes called from the front room. 'Ya missing the tele.'

Hakim walked inside.

'I bin waitin' for ya luv.' Agnes patted the settee.

'I am a lucky bugger.' Hakim sat down.

It seemed to Mr Smallwood that no matter how hard he tried, all his good work would be undone in the week between lessons.

How do you do would be replaced with howyagoin'.

Goin', comin', doin' seein' and strewth replaced the Queens English and every dropped 'g' was a thorn in Mr Smallwood's side. He blamed the television for the drop in standards.

Idiom, shmidiom, he was heard to say to his teaching colleagues. He wanted just one night where someone didn't ask him, 'ja'aveagoodweekend?'

After two months of lessons, Don Smallwood felt his small band of pupils had enough of a grasp of the language to give a small talk on their journey to Australia. He felt the autobiographical nature of the talk would make the class feel at ease.

The week before he had given them the task of preparing and now his eight pupils, dwindled down from the first flush of seventeen sat and tried to look anywhere but at him.

Miss Gombombo fidgeted with her paper and caught the teacher's eye.

She stood up and walked the walk of death to the front of the class and gave a nervous giggle.

Her story was short, succinct and over in 28 words.

'Thank you Miss Gombombo.' She scurried to her chair and sat down.

'Mr Peche?' Mr Smallwood smiled at the large fellow.

His tale was akin to a James Bond movie. In fact, Mr Smallwood recognised quite a few plagiarized phrases. The class were in awe of the derring-do and clapped when he finished.

Mr Stravinska stood up and bowed to the class. He went to the door and opened it and with a furtive glance looked down the corridor.

'Er, Mr Stravinska?'

'Sorry.' The man was a nervous wreck. He wiped his brow with his hanky and looked at the pupils.

His talk was of life-threatening situations, death, and more than once he drew his finger across his throat. Mr Peche felt he had been outdone and sat with a sullen look on his face.

Hakim would need to pull out all the stops to keep his audience enthralled after Stravinska's yarn.

Mr Smallwood felt for his throat and then checked the door.

Hakim rubbed his sweaty hands on his trousers. He felt a lump in his throat the size of a boiled egg waiting for his name to be called.

The time arrived and he stood up and walked slowly to the front of the class.

'G'day.' Mr Smallwood cringed.

'I got a bit of a yarn to tell ya, an' I reckon it's all dinkum.' Hakim swallowed.

Reg, Gwen, Lance, and half the Centennial patrons had put Hakim's yarn on some sound footing. If Mr Smallwood wanted to blame television, he was way off the mark.

'It all kinda started when I am drivin' taxi in Iran.'

'Er, it is driving Hakim.' Mr Smallwood made a simple correction.

160

Hakim got into his stride.

'I sees this bloke and he's sorta the wrong sorta bloke and I picked the bugger up.' Bak Van de Berg put his hands behind his head and sat back. He was enjoying himself.

Miss Gombombo brought her hand to her mouth to stifle an exclamation. Mr Smallwood died a thousand deaths.

.

'Blow me if he wasn't some sorta dodgy character. I had to up sticks and leg it. Thought I was gunna go to New Bloody Zealand, but I landed in Straya.' Hakim continued reading his notes in true Aussie fashion.

There were the bush fellas, the abo blokes, the home brew that could knock ya bloody socks off and the footy match. He ate at Arnolds and got a bloody house burger with the lot.

'Bloody good tucker,' Hakim added.

He launched into the episode of the fried food and Bluey chokin' a darkie in the public loos off the blacktop on the way to the big smoke 'cause his tough ol' bird was crook.

The class were mesmerized.

'I went to a barbie when I got 'ere and got pissed.'

'I'm workin' now, bustin' a gut an' earnin' a quid. It's hard yakka.'

'I'm one lucky bugger.' Hakim smiled and went to his seat. He turned to the class,

'An' I got a pan licker. I called her beaut. She's a ripper mate.' Hakim folded his paper and looked at his captive audience. They smiled and nodded. Not that they had an inkling of what Hakim had said, but it sounded confident, it sounded Australian and that had to count for something. Even Hakim wasn't sure on the finer details of his dissertation.

'Er, thank you Hakim.' Mr Smallwood sat back in his seat and broke his chalk in two.

Sylvia Rentree sat down and listened while Hakim talked about his day. He rubbed Beaut's ear and covered the incident of the kitchen sink in true Aussie style and soon had his audience in stitches.

'An' Reg had his finger stuck for about an hour,' he ended. Sylvia hung off his every word, his every dropped 'g' and his idioms. She looked up from her lamington and smiled. Hakim smiled back. Gwen gave Lance a jab in the ribs which made him drop his lamington.

'So, Hakim,' Sylvia began, 'I have been inquiring on your behalf. It seems you are wanted in Iran and as such the Australian Government have decided to …' Everyone sat on the edge of their seats.

'Have decided to offer you asylum.' Sylvia shuffled some papers and smiled at Hakim.

'So, he's legit?' Lance cut to the chase.

'Yes.' Sylvia nodded. 'I have all the papers here, and now he can proceed.'

'Proceed?' Hakim asked.

'Of course. You will be processed, managed, administered and directed.'

'Thanks.'

'Not a problem.' Sylvia opened her file and pulled out a pink form.

It transpired that the pink form was for a medical, the yellow form for the results of the medical, the blue form for the assessment of the yellow form and the magenta form … Sylvia looked at the magenta. 'Oh, sorry this is for vaccinations.'

There was the background check in triplicate, the statement of intent in black pen and the qualifications attained in small print.

Hakim looked at the mountain of paperwork.

'Bloody hell.'

Sylvia fished about in her handbag and came up with a pen.

'Just one more thing.'

Hakim looked at the pile of papers in front of him.

'Tax.'

The word sent Lance into a spin. He grabbed the table for support.

'Tax?'

'That's right. You will need to register with the ATO.'

'Don't do it mate.' Lance grabbed Hakim's arm.

'What is ATO.'

'They're the devil. They get their claws into ya and never let go.'

'Mr Cracknell, a good Australian citizen relishes the opportunity to pay tax,' Sylvia said. Lance nearly had an apoplexy. Sylvia slid the pile of papers over to Hakim. 'You can do it online if you'd prefer. Once you get a TFN then you can get super and you'll be set.'

'TFN. Super?' Hakim picked up the pen and twiddled it in his fingers.

'Yes. That's it.' Sylvia might be from the left of centre when it came to politics, but she knew who paid her wages and where the money came from. The public service ran on solid foundations of fiscal management, so did Sylvia's bank balance.

Ms Rentree left with a Tupperware container of lamingtons, the recipe for said lamingtons and a knitting pattern for bed socks.

'I like her.' Gwen said as she washed the dishes while Lance looked on.

'I like her.' Hakim added. Gwen smirked at Lance and winked.

Reg listened as they sat in the shade of a eucalyptus tree at smoko as Hakim told him about the paperwork.

'I have bloody heaps.'

'Strewth.'

'And the ATO.'

The acronym made Reg choke on his flavoured milk.

'This is bad?'

'Bloody crook mate.'

'ATO.' Hakim said it again and Reg broke out into a sweat.

'Look, I got a mate. Sweet as a nut. He'll set ya straight. He's straight up.'

'He is the ATO?' Hakim asked.

'Not bloody likely.' Reg finished his sausage roll and brushed the crumbs from his beer gut. 'I'll give him a bell and we'll swing by this arvo.'

Hakim nodded. He had no idea what Reg had said, but it sounded ok.

Stanley Dunning had an office above a Chinese restaurant which was run by a large Chinese family who gave him discount for cooking their books.

He sat with the air-con flat out and put it straight to Reg and Hakim.

'Look, I can do the odd little bit of deductions. You know me Reg, the odd little bit. But this, he spread his hands over Hakim's forms. 'This is the ATO, know what I mean.'

'Jeez, I just thought that …'

'Sorry mate. I know he's a mate of yours an' all, but this is reffo stuff an' I don't wanna get into deep shit. Know what I mean. 'Stan wiped the sweat from his face with a flaccid handkerchief and sat back in his chair.

'Ya see Stan, it's like this.' And Reg told him about the sheila with the coloured hair, the grant money he was receiving for Hakim, the grant money he wasn't returning for Hakim and the PAYE he wasn't returning for Hakim, well, it was quite a bit of a mess. Honesty comes in all shapes and sizes. Reg was about a size 48 with a bit of that Aussie larrikin streak that makes just about anything fair game.

'Ah.' Stan looked at Reg. Reg looked at Hakim and grinned. 'An' now he's gonna be official and all that and he's been bustin' a gut for me an' all that and well it's kinda like, well, I gotta get it sorted.'

'Ah.' Stan nodded. 'And when did he start?'

'Jeez it was kinda someit like, kinda about 3 months or someit.'

'Not today?'

'Nah.' Reg shook his head.

'Today.' Stan said with some emphasis.

'Nah. Three months or someit.'

'TODAY.'

They all sat in silence. Hakim smiled at Stan. Stan looked at Reg. Reg looked at Hakim.

'Yeah, I recollect it was just today.' Reg cottoned on.

'Ah.'

They looked at Hakim and the paperwork on his lap.

'I'll just take a squiz at these,' Stanley said. 'Leave 'em with me mate.'

'Thanks Stan. Knew you'd think of someit.'

Australians might have a neighbour they hate, they might be caught up with the mafia, they might owe money to Radio Rentals, but all this pales in comparison to the terror the Australian Tax Office can instil with just one letter.

'Sorted.' Reg lined up the beers.

'This one's my shout mate.'

'Cheers.'

With his paperwork well underway, his job secured, and his night classes giving him the opportunity to drink with Bak, life was pretty good. On a fine evening when the crickets were in song, the sun was setting and the mosquitos hadn't left home for their takeaway, Hakim and Lance were sitting on the front verandah and enjoying a beer.

They looked over the trimmed front yard, the fence that had been fixed and given a lick of paint, the gate that now swung without squealing and the tended roses.

'Not bad eh?'

'Not bad.' Hakim said.

'Ya miss ya home Hakim?'

'Yeah. I miss a lot of things.'

'Like what?' Lance was ready to relax and listen.

'I miss my mother's cooking.'

'Yeah. I can understand that.' Lance glanced down at his belly.

'I miss Bluey.'

'Yeah. He's a top bloke.'

The men sat back and enjoyed the twilight. A beer, a mozzie coil and the tele's blue light giving the verandah a tinge of the exotic.

Somewhere in the house the telephone rang. They heard Gwen pick up and a muffled conversation ensued.

'Ya think ya wanna stay in Straya?'

Hakim considered the question. He was safe. Life was good. He enjoyed his work, but something was missing.

'Dunno.'

'Ya know ya family now mate.'

'Ta.'

'Ya know we'd stick by ya, don'tcha?' Lance cracked another coldie.

'Yeah.'

'So whydon'tcha. Stay I mean.'

'I …'

'What you need is a sheila.' Lance felt he had a handle on the male psyche.'

'I dunno Lance.' Hakim rubbed the back of his neck and shook his head. Women were trouble. Woman wanted things. They wanted your time, money and to meet your mother. The next thing you know they are dragging you around to pick out throw cushions and kettles. Hakim wondered if he was ready for throw cushions. Reg had schooled him on the perils of women. Reg, having had three wives, thought he knew a thing or two about women and their wants.

'Look mate. Leave it ta me.' Lance sat back after his far-reaching pronouncement. Lance was all for being a can-do man, so long as someone else was doing the 'do' part.

'I know,' Lance sat up. 'What about that sheila, you know, Sylvia.'

'Sylvia?' Hakim took a drink. She was nice. She was educated. She had his best interests at heart, but she was a feminist. A strident feminist. Hakim heard Reg's words echoing in his ear,

'They wanna change ya mate, and it ain't for the best. Watch out. If she wants ta put ya in a polo shirt, don't do it. If she wants to see ya baby photos, don't do it.' Reg felt he'd been through the ringer and only just managed to come out the other side.

'What about Sylvia?' Gwen came to the front door after the phone call.

'Ah, nuthin' luv. Just talking.' Lance winked at Hakim.

Gwen stood in the doorway, 'You'll never guess who that was on the blower.'

'Nah.' Lance said.

'It was Blue.'

'Ya shittin' me.'

'Nope. It was Blue alright.' Gwen said.

'We were just talkin' about Blue. Weren't we just talking about Blue, Hakim?'

'Too right.'

'Well ya never guess what he said.'

'Nah.' Lance said.

'Well he rang and you'll never guess.' Gwen said shaking her head.

'What woman? What'd he say?'

'He's bloody gonna get hitched.'

'Ya shittin' me.' Lance choked on his beer.

'Hitched?' Hakim asked.

'Blue's getting married.'

And this is how it happened.

Bluey made the trip back to the Peninsular Bar and Grill in 10 hours flat. He had planned on a quick drink and then knock off the two-hour drive to the Station and his bunk, but when you have been to the big smoke and you rock up at the Peninsular B & G there is a lot to catch up.

The Peninsular Bar & Grill was neither on a peninsular or a grill, but Maylee thought it added a bit of class to have that funny little squiggle between Bar and Grill.

'The whole box and dice,' as Bill like to describe his wife's business acumen. 'She's got it – up top,' he'd often be heard to say. 'Cluey,' he'd add, if you were in any doubt.

Maylee came to Wallopi with big ideas. Bill had had a holiday – fell in love and that was that. All the nonsense about his mail order bride went straight over his head so many times it was like the flight path at Kingsford Smith airport. Maylee did come from Thailand, but she reckoned it was love at first sight. Ol' Bill couldn't argue with that. What the town folk all agreed upon was that Maylee was a bloody breath of fresh air to the previously named Drover's Way pub and Bill never seemed happier. Wallopi residents took to Maylee as a meat ant takes to a picnic.

Blue walked into the bar and the five men at the bar turned and gave him a wave.

'It's Blue.'

'Yeah. Blue.'

'Bloody Blue.'

'Mate, it's Blue.'

And Jocko said, just to get it all clear. 'I reckon it's Blue.'

'Howdy.' Blue walked to the bar and the barmaid, Gloria put a schooner of icy cold beer in front of him. He savoured the moment looking longingly at the beer, the condensation just starting to run down the side, the head, that frothy white, almost going over the rim.

Bluey picked up his pint and a hand whipped it away before it touched his lips.

'No beer for you.'

'What?' Blue looked at Maylee holding his beer at arm's length.

'No beer for you.'

'Please.' Blue was dying. His tongue was stuck to the roof of his mouth.

The other patrons looked on. This was something different. It beat looking at a beer mat any day.

'But …'

'You have Bill's choppers.' Maylee gave his beer to Gloria.

'Ya kiddin' me.'

'You stole Bill's choppers.'

If you have ever had that sinking feeling when you just know it's not going to turn out well, you will know how Bluey felt at this particular moment.

He had left Ralph unattended.

'Bloody Nora.' Blue pushed back his hat and tried to think, fast.

'I'll get 'em.' He was half way to the door when Maylee grabbed his arm.

'I'm coming.'

'No, really. It's all good. I'll just nip out. Won't be a sec.'

'I'm coming.'

The other drinkers moved to the window to get a better look.

Bill came into the bar and Gloria gave him the lowdown in a few words.

'Bloody hell.' Bill fell in behind his wife. It was a place he felt at home.

The procession followed Bluey outside.

There was a silent moment of thanks as Blue didn't see Ralph anywhere.

'You get the choppers now.' Maylee stood with her arms folded over her chest. Bill wished they were lost. He'd had an earful of the chastising about losing them in the first place.

'Bluey, ya got 'em alright.'

'Yeah.' Blue walked to the ute and just then Ralph popped up at the sound of his master's voice.

As I have said, Ralph has a dog's brain. What the attraction of a set of upper dentures is to a dog is anyone's guess, but there was no denying Ralph was smitten. He hung out of the driver's side window and had Bill's teeth in his mouth. That they were positioned perfectly was just a co-incidence, but a mighty funny one.

Bluey looked at Maylee. Maylee looked at Ralph. Ralph looked at Bill.

'I reckon they fit him better than me.' Bill said and began to laugh. His wife turned on her heels and walked back inside.

'Well, ya gotta see the funny side, don't cha.' Jocko said as he took his place at the bar.

Maylee gave him a stare that might have curdled milk.

174

'Ah, luv,' Bill trailed after his wife. 'They didn't fit anyway. I'll get a better set, honest.' Bill began to grovel.

'We'll go to the Big Smoke. Get a good set an' all that.'

Maylee turned to her husband, 'Promise?'

'Promise,' Bill said. It was a small word, but his get out of jail card on more than one occasion.

Blue plucked the teeth from Ralph and threw them in the bushes.

'Bloody Nora,' Ralph jumped out of the ute and went hunting.

Simmo came out onto the verandah and lit up a ciggie.

'That mutt of yours, he'd better watch it 'round 'ere.'

Bluey came up to the verandah, 'S'all clear in there?'

'Yeah.' Simmo puffed on his smoke. 'Pretty funny though.'

'Yeah.' The men chortled.

Blue opened the door and peeked inside. Gloria inclined her head and smiled. 'All clear.'

She put a new beer on the bar and Bluey grabbed it and it slid down without touching the sides.

'Bloody Nora, that was close.'

The regulars all nodded in agreement. Jocko uttered the one word that they all understood with incalculable meaning, 'Women.' He rolled his eyes.

Bluey was the kinda fella that knew when to keep his trap shut when it came to women.

Others at the B & G were free and easy with their pontification on the merits of women, not that Jocko thought they had many merits to speak of – he had four wives to attest to the fact that women and merits shouldn't be said the same breath.

No-one dared to look his way and mention women if they didn't want an ear bashing for a good hour. Slim wasn't far behind in the matter of women. He had a rather vulgar line,

'Women,' he'd say, finger pointing to the ceiling, 'If ya couldn't root 'em they'd be piled five high at the dump.' Not that Slim had a hope in hell of trying the verb. Rumour had it that Slim would die a virgin, such were his diabolical hygiene habits. His one 'joke' would elicit a withering stare from Gloria and a backhanded swat with the house flyswat. Slim was a slow learner, he'd been through at least four flyswats and one banning for three days when Gloria was in a bad mood. Bluey knew the value of keeping his trap shut.

The line was firmly drawn at the B & G by Gloria Gerkoff. She knew her place in the scheme of things and everyone else knew her place in the scheme of things. What Gloria says goes, was the maxim the patrons adhered to with, - on the whole – unwavering loyalty.

Of course, you can't have a bar and grill without a bit of argy-bargy and biffo on a Friday night and a right piss up at the end of the stock run to the auction yards, but all things considered, Gloria was the law. What Gloria said was the law and Gloria made the law.

Bill and Maylee were happy with the arrangement. Gloria was happy with the arrangement and that's all that mattered.

Gloria Gerkoff, the other side of 60, was the epitome of style. Whose style no-one was quite sure, but she had enough panache for the Peninsular B & G in Wollopi. Her greatest assets sat proudly atop the bar, most nights constricted with a size F cup and covered in an expanse of leopard print spandex. They were the downfall of many a punter with a few too many and a quick wit. Gloria's flyswat was lightning fast and could take out an ear before the victim had time to regret his smart remark. Once, the story goes, Gloria left a ringer with ringing in his left ear for a fortnight. If her knockers didn't catch your eye the mole nestled between the two was bound to illicit a remark – in the privacy of your room, or after a decent 200 clicks down the road.

The sun blushed mole was lovingly cocooned at the beginning of the Grand Canyon forever keeping a wary eye on proceedings.

Some women can carry off tight stretch black leggings and look like Audrey Hepburn in Breakfast at Tiffany's. Gloria Gerkoff was not one of them. Her figure tended to mirror the beer kegs she rolled to the back room. It was all up front so to speak and supported by a couple of pool cues. How the body went from pins to kegs was anyone's guess, and Gloria would never tell, although if you ask Bill when he's been toting up the takings with a gin or three, he might wink with a knowing smile. There was a whiff of something between the two when he still had his own teeth and Gloria was still a natural blonde, but that was a long time ago and who believes it anyway.

Her coiffure was a work of art. Gloria was one of those women who when they find a hairstyle that suits, stick with it. She stuck with it for nearly 35 years. Her bouffant style, piled high and over the years set with a blue, sometimes pink tinge is the one thing that can be relied upon to never change, that, and also her unwavering sense of sarcasm, which goes with the territory of working as a barmaid in the B & G for 36 years. If you want a smart remark, you'd be in the wrong place. If you want something that can cut a man down to size in the time it takes to pour a shot of rum, Gloria is your man – or woman to be more politically correct.

If Slim had a vocabulary that was bigger than a beer bottle label he'd describe Gloria as formidable. Jacko, who thought his vocabulary on a par with that fellow Theo dinasorus would say she was formaldehyde. He was perfantic about his pacific intellectual capacitators, although if the wind was right he was ferdantic, it was a moot point.

When the dust had settled and Bluey had downed the first of many he began to relax in familiar surroundings when Gloria sidled up to him and smiled.
'So, Blue, how's ya mum?'
'Ah, she's a tough ol' bird. She'll be right.'
'What was it then?' Gloria asked as she wiped the bar.

Now here's the thing. When you are in familiar surroundings your guard is often left at the door. Bluey had left his in the ute and said,
'She's had an op for piles. Runs in the family.' As soon as the words had left his lips he regretted them. He tried to change the subject, but his powers of conversation had deserted him. He looked at the ceiling, the mirror over the cigarette machine, the bar, anywhere but at Gloria.
'So what'd they do Blue?' Slim asked. There is nothing like a private conversation at the B&G.

'They bloody hack 'em off.' Jocko entered the debate. 'You got 'em too eh?'

Bluey took a long swig of beer. His eyes roamed over the room.

'I bet yours are the size of grapes.' Jocko said, 'seein' that beer gut ya got there.'

'Like grapes are they, hanging out ya backside are they?' Slim asked. Blue squirmed on the seat.

'Yeah, he's got 'em alright.' Jocko pronounced as if he had Dr. on his drivers licence.

'She ok now Blue?' Gloria asked giving him another beer.

'Yeah. Right as rain.'

'I gotta go in for an op.' Jocko said.

The punters at the bar all looked at him with disbelief.

'Ya kiddin' me.'

'Nope.'

'Ya never serious Jocko?'

'Yep.'

'Jeez.'

'Too right.'

'Go on then. Whatchagot?' Gloria rolled her eyes.

Jocko took centre stage, a position he was familiar with and began.

'Well, ya know I had me prostrate out. Bloody big op that one was. The sheilas cried that day I'm tellin' ya.

They had all heard the story of Jocko's *prostrate*, Gloria going so far as to ask if he took it lying down.

Slim sat forward on his bar stool. He had a very small memory capacity and if he'd heard it before, he didn't remember it.

'Jeez Jocko. Slim sipped his beer.

'Yeah, well the doc said, mate, he said ya old fellas gonna have a bit of a rest.'

'Ya dad then?' Slim asked.

179

'Nah,' Jocko sighed. 'The halitosis was not good the doc said.'

'Prognosis?' Gloria proffered.

'Yeah.' Jock continued. He hitched up his shorts and picked apiece of peanut from his tooth.

'I had to break a few hearts.'

'Strewth,' Slim said. 'So what's up now Jocko?'

' I was all clear and now, well, I'm tellin' ya, the big C never leaves ya alone. Not when ya had it.'

'Crikey.' Slim said, 'how'd ya know?'

'I could feel me testostolones in me balls. Ache somethin' bad. Doc said so too. They take the hypocritical oath ya know. They can't just leave ya to die.'

'Never.'

'Too right. Someit bad.' Jocko passed his empty glass over to Gloria and she gave him another beer.

'So then what?' Blue asked.

'Well I got it here,' he pointed to his temple and there was a gasp from his audience. He tapped his head.

'No.'

'Yeah. Gotta go for an op.'

Gloria's eyes widened. She searched Jocko's face for an inkling of hyperbole, but he was serious for once.

'Jocko, mate.' Blue shouted him a beer.

'Ta. Ya know who ya mate's are.'

'So what's the doc say?' Slim patted Jocko's back.

'The prog, prog, prognoises?'

'Yeah.' Blue nodded.

'Well, we all gotta go sometime eh?'

'Yeah.' Slim went to the gents out the back.

They sat there looking at the bar, the news of Jocko's brain tumor a devastating blow to the regulars, when the phone rang.

Gloria picked up.

'Ya in luck, he's here now.' She beckoned Blue to the receiver. She put her hand over the mouthpiece, 'It's for you Bluey.'

'Me?'

'Yeah.' She shrugged. The punters listened in.

'Blue here.' He nodded. He looked at the regulars. 'Yeah.' He picked a peanut off the bar and popped it in his mouth. 'Yeah.' He looked at this face in the mirror. 'Nah.' Blue wasn't much of conversationalist. 'Right'o.' He put the phone down.

The other looked inquiringly at him.

'It was me boss.' Blue said then added, 'Nev.'

'What'd he say?' Slim asked. He wasn't up on the need for privacy when on the phone. He didn't own a phone and could count on one hand the number of calls he'd had in his adult life. Gloria raised the flyswat and Slim backed away, 'Just askin'. That's all.'

'I just got a bit of a break.'

'Whatdayamean?' Slim couldn't help himself. He dodged the swat.

'Cricket's got Chicken pox. I haven't had 'em. I got ta stay away for a few days the doc says.'

'Never.'

'Too right.' Blue nodded to Gloria and she gave him a beer.

'Where ya gonna stay Blue?' Gloria asked. 'Only I got a bed at my place if ya stuck.'

Jocko and Slim smirked and Slim jabbed Jocko in the ribs with is elbow.

'If ya stuck.' Gloria said.

'Ta.' Blue tipped back his hat and scratched his head. He watched Gloria disappear out the back and blew out a sign of relief.

'Ya gonna stay with Gloria then?' Slim asked.

181

'I'd rather glue me nut sack to a bullet train.' Blue looked at the entrance to the bar in case Gloria came back.

'She's keen eh?'

'Ya reckon?' Bluey shook his head.

'Yeah. Real keen Blue.' Slim smiled and gave his audience the full delights of his rotten three front teeth.

'I guess I could stay here.' He knew the B&G used to have rooms.

'They got 'em all right.' Slim said. 'I seen 'em once.'

Gloria came back with a fresh tea towel and wiped the bar.

'It'd be no trouble Blue. No trouble at all.'

'I dunno. P'raps they got rooms here.'

'I'll get Bill.' Gloria rang upstairs and Bill came tromping down the stairs.

'Blue wants ta know if ya got any rooms Bill?' Slim took over the proceedings. 'He's gotta stay in town on account of Crickets got the pox or someit.'

Bill frowned and looked to Bluey for some sense.

'I gotta stay in town on account of Cricket's got the chicken pox. Doc says so.'

'You got rooms Bill?' Gloria asked.

'We got one, I think it's still got a bed in it.'

'I got a nice spare room Blue. Real nice and clean.' Gloria wiped the bar and smiled in his direction.

'I'll ask Maylee.' Bill went upstairs.

'It'll be no trouble Blue. It's for free.'

Slim looked at Jocko and tried to keep a straight face.

Blue blew out a sigh, squirmed on his seat and began to study the wet beer coaster. Bill reappeared.

'Nah. We got nuthin' now.' What Bill neglected to explain was Maylee had said in no uncertain terms Bluey couldn't staying. If he steals a man's teeth, the glasses in the bar weren't safe.

Blue took a long drink for courage. He looked at Gloria, then at Jocko and Slim.

'A'right.'

'Want some glue Blue?' Jocko cracked up laughing.

'What's so funny?' Slim asked.

'Glue, you know. Glue.' Jocko said pointing to Blue.'

'Yeah. So. Glue?'

'Ah forgetit.' Jocko rolled his eyes at Slim. His mate's mental capacity was at its limit.

'So you'll be here for the 'do' then?' Bill said.

'Yep. He'll be here.' Gloria said. At least Bill could go back upstairs with some good news.

Bluey felt he needed some fortification if he was going to stay at Gloria's place. He put a wad of notes behind the bar, Gloria frowned and chewed the inside of her cheek with a quizzical look.

'Are you sure Blue?'

'Yep.'

'Really, only, it's just that you've already had a few.'

'Not a problem.'

Jocko and Slim watched the exchange and nodded. With the benefit of a spectator they could see the subtilties of the relationship that was forming.

Gloria poured another for Blue and if you had listened closely you might have heard a tisk. It was a small click of her tongue but it had far reaching repercussions.

Gloria Gerkoff was of Polish heritage and as anyone who has known a Pole in a social occasion or had the pleasure to be house guest, hospitality equals food. If you get out alive without putting on 4 kilos you're not in a Polish household.

The Peninsular Bar & Grill shut up shop on the dot of 11pm and Blue shuffled about on the verandah waiting for Gloria to appear. Ralph hopped in the ute and waited and presently a small white Hyundai Getz pulled out of the car park and the headlights flicked.

Gloria leaned out of the driver's window. 'Get in, you're over the limit.'

'Nah, she's right.' Blue hung onto the ute for moral support.

'Blue. Get in.' Gloria said with a little more force.

'S'ok.' Blue said. Ralph barked. 'I got Ralph. How about I just kip here t'night and see ya in the mornin'?'

'I'm tellin' you one last time. Get in or I'll ring ya bloody neck.'

'Ok. Ok. But Ralph's gotta come too.'

A Hyundai Getz isn't the biggest of cars. Ralph sat on the back seat and his head lolled between the front seats.

'He's me mate.' Blue patted the head and kissed it.

'Does he need to huff on me like that.' Gloria shooofftied to one side and drove through the town.

'He's me mate.' The cool night air often has the effect of making alcohol go straight to your head. Blue's brain was about 70% proof.

'I love me mate.' He hugged Ralph and Ralph began to jump about.

'Bluey, I can't drive with him all over me.'

'He likes ya Gloria.'

'Well he can like me from a distance.' Gloria checked her hair in the mirror and turned into a small cul-d-sac.

'Here we are.' She parked on the footpath and cut the lights.

Blue followed her to the front door and smiled, 'Ralph and me can just kip 'ere.'

'Bluey. Listen to me. I have a lovely little spare room. The dog can sleep outside on the patio.'

'A'right.' Blue had passed the 'love my mate' stage and gone straight to 'anything you say is ok by me' phase.

He followed like a lamb to the slaughter into Gloria's humble little home and was deposited at the small kitchen table with matching chairs.

'I'll just get you a snack.' Gloria put on her frilly apron and busied herself in the kitchen.

It was all too much for Blue. He'd been travelling all day, he'd had a few too many beers. He passed out on the kitchen table and woke up to pickled cabbage and smoked sausage.

'You can't go to bed on beer.'

'I can't?' Blue said. It was news to him.

'Eat.'

'Nah, she's right Gloria. I'll just kip 'ere.'

'Eat.' It wasn't a request.

Blue picked up his fork.

The sun hit Bluey like a sledgehammer and he rolled over before his eyeballs started to scream. A moan escaped from his mouth and he wasn't sure he was even human. His eyes cracked open and were assaulted with yellow flowers on brown curtains and gold striped flock wallpaper. He felt strangely sick and burped. It tasted of sausages.

'Bluey?' A voice wafted over his consciousness.

'Ghhhhhhth.' Bluey tried to make his tongue work.

'Do you want some breakfast?'

'Ghhhhhth.' Blue tried to find some spit to get a word or two straight.

'I'm coming in.'

This got the ol' grey matter sparking. Bluey suddenly remembered where he was, why he was there, how he got there and who was on the other side of the door. It came in a flash and he jumped out of bed, only to discover he was in his jocks. You'd be hard pressed to see an Olympic athlete move as quick as Blue and disappear under the sheet.

Gloria entered with a smile and a tray of food. '

'I thought you'd be hungry luv.' She put the tray on the bedside table and straightened the napkin.

'Thanks.' Bluey pulled the sheet up to his neck and scratched his prickly chin.

'I've made lunch. I hope you like quiche.'

'Quiche?'

'Hmmm.' Gloria twiddled with her ribbon belt.

'I can wash your clothes if you like.' Gloria looked at the pile of clothes on the floor and pulled her housecoat a little tighter over her chest.

'Nah, she's right Gloria. I got some others in the ute.'

'It's no trouble, I'm doing a load Bluey.' Gloria picked up the stubbies and singlet and walked out.

Now Bluey was trapped. With no clothes he was a prisoner. He looked at the breakfast.

'Bird food,' he said to himself. Muesli and yogurt with seeds scattered on top. What he thought he needed was something like an Arnold burger.

He pecked at the bowl and then remembered he had a dog. Ralph would eat anything.

The wardrobe presented Gloria's sartorial elegance in all its glory. Blue picked a frilly thing that fitted, just, over his gut and tied with a bow. It was leopard print which only added to the eye catching effect.

He tiptoes to the door and listened, then snuck out and found the back door, via the kitchen. A quick glance at the clock revealed it was 11am. Ralph would be starving.

Bluey opened the door to the patio and bumped into a lad up a ladder.

'Bloody Nora.' Blue pulled his leopard kimono a little tighter over his chest

'What the ...' The bloke shimmied down the ladder and looked at Blue. Cristos & Son were installing solar panels. They didn't expect to see a cross dresser.

'Jeez. Hey Dad, take a gander at this.' Mr Cristos took a look.

'Crikey.'

'It's not what it looks like mate.' Bluey said.

'A'right then. What is it?'

'She's got me clothes. I'm a bloody prisoner.'

'Never.' Young Cristos was one of those lads who is an avid reader of crime fiction. 'A prisoner.'

'Yeah.'

'Ya escapin' then?' Mark Cristos asked.

'Nah, tryin' to find me dog.'

This line of logic escaped the tradies.

'He's called Ralph.'

'So, ya a prisoner of this lady, and she's got ya dog too.'

'Yeah.'

'An' ya trying to escape but ya won't go without ya dog called Ralph.'

'Yeah.' Bluey couldn't see the problem.

'Jeez.' Mark thought he was onto something. 'Ya think of ringing the police.'

'For a missing dog?' Bluey asked.

Ralph rescued the moment by bounding into the group and jumping up on Bluey. His claws snagged the nylon kimono and pulled more than one or two threads.

'Now I'm in for it.' Bluey tried to pull Ralph off.

'She gonna torture you?'

'What?' Blue was trying to calm Ralph when he spied the new red collar around his neck. Then a glance around the patio and he saw three bowls with their intended contents in big letters. Water, food, biscuits.

Gloria had been homemaking.

'So ya gonna make a run for it?' Mark was hoping for some excitement.

'Whatyaonabout?' Bluey said.

'Escape.' Mark expounded.

'Nah, she's made me lunch.'

The Cristos family knew all about lunch. Bluey's simple statement had explained the situation and finalized the conundrum.

'Oh, right then.' The matter was settled. The team of Cristos & Son went for smoko and Bluey whipped back inside and was headed for the spare room when Gloria caught him in the act.

'Bluey,' she said and used her feminie whiles to great effect.

'I was just … well, Ralph … and I was …' Blue tried to form a cogent argument but it wasn't happening. He was mightily distracted by Gloria. She was wearing a small (ish) top that covered her assets -just- and a pair of black bike pants that knew the value of lycra stretch.

'You sit yourself down Blue and I'll make you something to eat.' Gloria ran by the maxim that the way to a man's heart was through his stomach. Her mother had taught her well and she set to work in the kitchen. Blue sat at the table and watched her work. She was, he decided quite pleasing to the eye.

But to be honest, when you have had the life of a ringer and only seen the back end of a horse, a sheep, a cow and on the odd occasion a shearer in the shower, Gloria was beauty personified.

'Ya don't need to go to any trouble Gloria.'

'No trouble Blue. No trouble at all.' She set the table and fussed with a napkin and matching tablecloth.

'I'm useta doin' for meself.' Bluey said.

'Oh, don't you worry about that.' Gloria replied.

'A man could get used to this.' Blue sat back and wiped the egg off his face. Gloria chalked one up on her score board.

'Now, I hope you don't mind Blue, but I just thought that mutt of yours would appreciate the woman's touch.'

'I saw that. Ta very much.'

'Ralph isn't it?'

'Yeah. He's smart ya know. He's knows a good sort when he sees one.' Blue looked at his hostess. 'So do I.'

'Oh, Bluey.' Gloria blushed and pushed her hair in place, brushed a crumb off her apron and if I am any judge, went all coy.'

After a second cuppa and a piece of cake Blue retired to his bedroom to find his clothes washed and pressed and neatly folded on his made bed. He'd never seen ironed stubbies before and marvelled at the creases. His blue singlet and shirt had similar treatment. He thought he'd see it all until he went into the bathroom.

A blue towel with a new toothbrush awaited him and a bottle of Old Spice completed the ensemble.

He emerged from the shower feeling like a new man. His shave was close, his hair brushed, his nostril hair trimmed and his fingernails clean. Once dressed he looked like an advertisement for the working man. He felt a million dollars.

He was admiring himself in the mirror when Gloria knocked.

'Blue, I have a split shift today. I'm going to work,' Gloria said through the door.

Blue opened the door and grinned from ear to ear.

'I'll come too.' He could think of no better way to spend an afternoon than at the B & G.

'Are you sure?'

'Too right.'

The lunchtime crowd at the B & G was thin. Jocko and Slim were fixtures, the odd traveller came in on the odd occasion and then there was R & C at 1:15 on the dot, every day, Monday to Friday without fail.

Bluey strolled into the bar and Jocko nudged Slim with his elbow.

'G'day.'

'Looks like ya going to a wedding or a funeral,' Slim said nodding in Bluey's direction.

'Wotdayamean?'

'Ya could cut yaself on them creases Blue.' Jocko pointed to his ironed stubbies.

'Git.' Blue sat down and began to ruminate on how he had been so easily led.

'So, Jocko, hows the, ya know?' Blue asked tapping his temple. 'I'll shout ya a drink.'

'Ta.' Jocko touched his head and frowned. 'Mate.'

'Mate.'

'The op's tomorra.'

'Jeez.' Blue shook his head. 'Bloody bad luck eh.'

'Mate.'

'Mate.'

Commraderie is like that.

'When ya mate's down and got the big C nuthin' is too much trouble.' Slim said while supping his beer. Slim even got as far as suggesting a meat raffle, so long as he didn't supply the meat, organise the tickets, count the takings, buy the get-well card or anything that might involve work.

The bar was quiet as Jocko supped his shouted beer.

'Mate,' Slim wiped his glassy eyes. They sat in silence for a bit when a stranger blew in and walked to the bar. The three men looked him over, decided on the spot that his was dinkum and waited to see what he would drink.

'I'll have a beer please.'

'Which one luv?' Gloria asked pointing to the taps.

'This,' the stranger pointed to a XXXX.

This choice given the nod of approval the bloke sat down next to Jocko.

'Mate.'

'Mate.' Just the usual exchange.

Slim looked at Gloria. Gloria looked at Blue and Blue looked at Slim.

Jocko had found fresh meat.

I should explain that Jocko is one of life's experts. He's a been there, done that type of bloke who can spin a yarn about his 'done that' that would put the makers of sleeping pills to shame.

He launched into his time directional boring – the boring bit Gloria and Slim had heard before, many times. Blue had only heard it twice, but that was enough. He tuned out and watched Gloria at the bar. She worked with effortless efficiency he thought.

After three beers the young man asked the time. Jocko was on a roll and sidestepped the enquiry when the subject got around to his op.

'Oh, really, where?' the stranger asked.

'Here,' Jocko pointed to his temple.

'That's a sunspot.'

'Doc said somethin' 'bout that. I gotta have somethin' called a biodegradable or somethin'.'

'A biopsy?'

'Yeah, that's it.'

Slim, Blue and Gloria looked like stunned mullets.

'Sun spot?' Gloria said.

'A bloody sunspot.' Blue reiterated.

'Yeah, mate.'

'A bloody fuckin' sun spot.' Slim nearly fell off his bar stool.

'Yeah.'

Jocko moved onto his New Guinea experiences as the others were lost for words.

The young lad looked to Gloria for rescue when the door opened on the dot of 1:15 and Rupert, with Crispin not far behind, walked through the door.

Rumour has it that Rupert and Crispin were on the run from Sydney's underworld. Whether it had more to do with the re-runs of Perry Mason no-one knew, but the rumour persisted. What was a fact was that Rupert and Crispin were the best hairdressers in Wollopi. In fact, they were the only hairdressers in Wollopi and to quote Jocko, they were as gay as a carnival.

But as with all small towns they became part of the fabric of the community and aside from their outrageously camp behaviour, they were part and parcel of Wollopi.

Rupert winked at Gloria, 'the usual hun.' The usual was a cherry daiquiri. Gloria nipped out the back and shaved some ice off the freezer wall, picking out the odd pea and returned to the bar to concoct the cocktail. Jocko, and Slim and Blue watched the performance in awe of her skill. She sliced, swished and ended with a little umbrella.

'Can I 'ave one of them?' Slim asked.

'Bend over,' Gloria said without breaking her concentration.

Rupert sipped. 'Spot on girl.'

'I'll have my G & T Gloria.' Crispin said.

'You all ready for the do?' Gloria went to work.

'Wouldn't miss it for the world.'

'Maylee's been hard at it making about a thousand spring rolls and the like.' Gloria rolled her eyes to the ceiling indicating the floor above the bar.

The 'do' was billed as an event. Events of any kind were thin on the ground in Wollopi They had the usual bingo, school dance, footy and Father Christmas, but something out of the ordinary was, well, out of the ordinary.

'We'll be over there,' Rupert waved his hand in the direction of their seats, and they retired to the only booth in the bar. Its red plush velvet seats pocked marked with a thousand cigarette burns and the back rest a dirty shade of hell from numerous bodies.

Jocko began his dissertation on the merits of cooking, not that he knew much about it, but what he did know stretched to another two beers. The young man sloped off to the dunny in the hope of never hearing about what oil to

193

use, New Guinea or directional boring in his lifetime. It was the appearance of Bill that halted Jocko.

'Ya seen a young bloke in here yet?'

'Yeah.' Slim answered. 'He's taking a slash.'

'He's the in-ter-net bloke.'

'Jeez.' Slim looked at the toilets as if they were the portal to Narnia.

'The do's tomorra ya know.'

'Tomorra?'

'Yeah. We got the dish an' everythin'. They came last week. Did someit on the roof and wires and stuff. It's all bloody go here ya know.'

'Jeez.' Slim was lost for words. A regular occurrence.

'I knew a bloke on the in-ter-net once.' Jocko said, taking Bill's pronunciation.

'It's bloody everywhere. Everyone knows a bloke Jocko.' Blue said.

Jeremy Swindon opened the toilet door and groaned. He took a deep breath and walked to the bar with a purposeful air and grabbed his change to head out the door when Bill collared him.

'You the in-ter-net bloke?'

'Pardon?'

'You the in-ter-net bloke?' Bill said again.

'Err, yes. From Telecom.'

'I'm Bill.' Bill held out his meaty hand.

'Jeremy Swindon.'

The crowd looked on. Nothing is private in a small country town.

Jeremy smiled as Jocko explained he'd be away for the do because of his op.

'That's a shame.' Jeremy said.

'Never mind.' Gloria poured Bluey a beer and added, 'on me luv.'

'Ta luv.' Blue was feeling mellow towards his fellow man and woman.

'Can ya get to I-ran on the internet.'

'Sure.' Jeremy wondered if he had stepped back into the wardrobe and was in Narnia after all. These people were seriously out of touch. He speculated if they had heard of snap chat.

'So, I could just get I-ran and talk to people an' stuff.'

'Of course.'

'An' they could see me an' stuff, like video and stuff.'

'Yes.' Jeremy couldn't make it any plainer.

'What's it all about luv?' Gloria leaned on the bar and looked at Bluey.' He copped an eyeful of Gloria's many charms.

'Well ...' and then they heard all about Hakim. Naturally the snake was about to strike, the ute was almost irreparable, the dirt track unpassable, Plinthe Hill – well we all know about Plinthe Hill, and by the time Bluey had finished Crispin, Rupert, Jocko, Slim, Jeremy and Bill were open-mouthed.

'And this fellow is from Iran you say?' Crispin asked.

'Yeah, top bloke too. He's with me sister now, gettin' his papers and stuff.'

'An' he thought he was in New Bloody Zealand eh?' Slim chuckled.

'You didn't even know where you were the other night ya drongo.' Jocko said.

'Ah, get outta here.'

'Nah, you get outta here.' Jocko stood up and put up his fists.

'Quit it.' Gloria brought out her fly swat and gave Slim a swish. He forgot to duck.

'And will we meet this fellow?' Rupert asked.

'Dunno.' Blue frowned.

'I miss the bugger ya know. He was good for a laugh.'

'You could skype him.' Jeremy offered.

'What?'

'Skype. It's talking on the internet with face contact.'

'Yeah, that'd be good. I dunno though.' Blue said. '

'Look, do you have a number.' Jeremy brought out his smart phone with umpteen gigabytes and world satellite connectivity on a three year plan that cost as much as a small house mortgage. It was his must have item.

'I dunno. Hang on.' Blue looked to Gloria. 'You might have a number. She rang here remember?'

Gloria looked at the scratch pad next to the phone. It still had Gwen's number at the top. There wasn't much telephoning in the Bar & Grill.

Jeremy dialled up and waited for the pick up.

'Hello?'

'Hello. Bluey wants to talk to you.' Jeremy handed over his phone to Blue while watching his every move. It was akin to a hostage swap where one side is loathed to let go before the other side does the same.

196

Usually Blue isn't stuck for words. But with someone else's phone to his ear, no time for his brain to kick in and everyone listening he couldn't think of anything to say.

'Errr.'

'Blue is that you Blue.'

'Errr.'

'Lance, I think it's Blue. He sounds like he's in pain. I think he's havin' a heart attack or someit.'

'Blue, Blue, stay calm. Breath luv. Are ya near the ute? Can ya crawl to the ute and get yaself to the docs?'

'Gwen.' Blue looked at his audience and gave a silly grin.

Now he needed to explain to his sister that he was in fact sitting up at the bar enjoying the hospitality of his mates with 4 beers under his belt. She wouldn't like it.

'Hello?' He fell back on the ol' I can't hear you trick and handed the phone back to the young whippersnapper.

'Hello?'

'Hello, is that the doc?'

'No, I'm from telecom.'

'Are ya near the doc.' Gwen asked.

'No. Um listen. I'm with Bluey and he would like to ring you tomorrow and skype.

'Skype?'

'Yes.'

'So he's not dying?'

'No.'

'So he's not having a heart attack?'

'No. He's at the bar.'

'Hello?' Jeremy looked at his phone. 'She seems to have hung up.'

'Dunno. Dodgy line or someit.' Blue supped his beer.

'Well, it better work tomorra.' Bill said.

Bluey drank his way through Gloria's shift without much effort. He made it as far as his ute and collapsed in the front seat for a kip. It was only when he rolled over and a scooter jabbed him in the ribs that he remembered his errand to Nellie.

'Bloody Nora.' He looked at the stuff he had bought. There was no way he would be able to get out to the compound and back by the do.

He was contemplating his dilemma when Jeremy Swindon came out onto the verandah for a smoke.

'Hey, mate.'

'Me?' Jeremy wasn't up with the vernacular of the bush.

'Yeah.' Blue beckoned the young man over.

'Ya got that phone of yours.'

'Pardon?' Jeremy didn't understand the question. Who would be *without* their phone. It was unthinkable.

'Ya got ya phone thingy?' Blue said pushing back his hat.

'Of course.' Jeremy grabbed his phone from his pocket.

'Ya reckon ya could ring Mungdeegi?'

'Where?'

'It's out Woop Woop. Bit further than the turn off.'

'Woop Woop?' Jeremy was at a loss. Living in the city will deprive you of an education, no matter how close you live to the State school.

'Jeez.'

'How do you spell it.' Jeremy readied his index finger.

Bluey tried his best. The pre-emptive text came up with a number of variations.

'Is this it?' Jeremy poked the phone in Bluey's direction.'

'Dunno, I don't have me glasses. Anyways it's a compound and I s'posed to deliver some stuff and stuff an' I was wantin' to ring and let 'em know that I can't do it for a bit and …' Blue trailed off as the sun beat down and he was getting hot.

'I have a Mungdeegi compound general store here.' Jeremy said.

'That's it.'

'So, you want me to ring?'

'Yeah.'

Jeremy wondered if anyone knew that the phone calls cost money. They seemed to take his largess for granted like it was fresh air or something.

He dialled and waited for a response.

'It's ringing,' he said to Blue who was beginning to sweat in the cab. Of course he could have stepped out of the cab, retreated to the verandah and the cool, but that would have required thought and action. The two were mutually exclusive.

'Hello.' Jeremy said.

'Hello?'

'I have Bluey here, he wants to talk to you.'

'Me?'

'Yes.'

'Why?'

'I don't know.'

'Well, why cant he tell me?'

'Pardon?'

'Why cant he talk to me?'

Jeremy rolled his eyes. He wondered if shop work in the air-conditioned centre might be preferable to these bushy types who didn't have a clue.

'Bluey.' Jeremy handed over his phone like he was giving away his first born.

'Hello?' Blue shouted.

'Is that you Blue?'

Yeah.'

'Mate.'

'Mate.'

It might have ended there except Jeremy poked Bluey in the shoulder. He was paying for the call after all.

'Oh, listen. It's Blue here.'

'Yeah.'

Mate.'

Jeremy gave Blue a bigger poke.

'Hang on a sec, I got this fella pokin' me.' Blue looked at Jeremy and the young fella backed off.

'Bluey.'

'Yeah.'

'Mate.'

'Well listen, I got some stuff and other stuff for Nellie. She's expectin' it.

'Yeah.'

'An' I can't get it to her just yet. So she'll need to wait.'

'A'right.'

'An' I'm gonna be in Wollopi for a bit so if she wants to get the stuff then she's gotta come to Wollopi or someit.'

'A'right.'

'Ok then.'

'Mate.

'Mate.' Bluey hung up and handed the phone back to Jeremy.

'Ta Mate.'

Jeremy rubbed the sweat from the screen on his trouser leg as Crispin and Rupert tottered out of the bar.

'Oh, darling, you can get cream for that.' Rupert said and they giggled down the steps and walked up the street to their salon.

When Bluey woke up he felt his afternoon was shaping up nicely. He drove his ute to Gloria's place and parked out the front, then found the key in the stone that is designed to stop people looking for the key, (which is readily available in any dollar shop, so the secret is out) and let himself in.

There was a sandwich in the fridge with his name on it; Gloria thought of everything. So, Bluey sat down on the sofa, turned the tele on, put his feet up and settled in until Gloria came home from work. *A bloke could get used to this*, he thought as he drifted off for another afternoon nap as Days of our Lives played out another life-threatening drama.

It wasn't until Gloria gently poked him in the arm that Bluey woke up to the smell of lamb chops.

'You looked beat, so I left you to it.' Gloria handed him a cold beer.

'Ta luv.' Bluey smiled and thought he might have just arrived in heaven. Gloria smiled at him and sat down with a soda water and lime.

'Blue,' Gloria crossed her legs and shuffled in a little closer.

'Yeah.' Blue sipped his beer.

'You know you can stay as long as you like.'

'Thanks.'

'And you know I like having you around.'

'Ta. I like being here.' Blue looked at the tele and his mind drifted to the merits of whiter than white socks.

'Blue,' Gloria fiddled with Blue's singlet.

'Yeah.'

'Do you really like being here?'

'Too right.' Blue took a swig of beer and wondered if the lamb came with mint sauce.

'I like you being here too Blue.'

'Do ya.'

'Of course.' Gloria began to use all her feminine wiles. She giggled, snuggled, battered her eye lids and licked her lips. Every trick in the book. Lucky for her Bluey hadn't read the book.

'You're a good sort Bluey. I've always said you're a good sort.'

'Did ya?'

'Of course.'

And then Bluey did something quite out of character. He leaned over and gave Gloria a small peck on the cheek. She responded by throwing her arms around his neck and just about taking out his tonsils with her tongue.

It would be a hard man who could resist Gloria when she got going. Bluey was made of marshmallow. He was putty in her hands.

To go into the details would be unkind. You could say it had been a long time between drinks. Gloria and Blue were human after all. Thirsty humans.

As so often happens when you have had a drink, the world becomes a nicer place. It might not be written all over your face, but a look in the mirror confirms that you feel fantastic.

202

Blue and Gloria basked in the afterglow, sitting at the kitchen table with a small pick and mix and a cup of tea; they were both on the other side of 50 after all. There was something in the air and they both breathed deeply.

'Blue.'

'Gloria.'

The Arnotts Biscuits were eaten over an unwritten, unsaid, pact of love. And it was love.

Why Bluey hadn't noticed how nice Gloria was all along was a mystery, but now he had righted a wrong. Why he didn't see that Gloria was a strikingly good woman before he couldn't say. Now he decided he could put that omission behind him.

'Gloria, ya a top sheila.'

'Oh, Blue.' Gloria traced the patterns on her tablecloth and blushed. 'You're not so bad yourself.'

Yep, it was definitely love.

The afterglow lingered as Bluey had a shower and changed into the clothes Gloria had laid out for him on his bed. He looked at the chino slacks, the shirt with little squiggles on it and the new jocks. He didn't like the look of the jocks. They had none of the usual things he was accustomed to and sported a wide elastic band and legs bits. He held them up and took a look. Such is the nature of love, one often overlooks the predilection of the other half, sometimes known as the better half. Blue put the underwear on and surveyed the result.

Some men can wear things without elastic, some can't. Blue was of the latter. Things that were kept corralled were roaming free. He walked a bit, stretched a bit and put on his stubbies. The short legged jocks hung about below his shorts. It wasn't a good look.

There comes a time when a man needs to put his foot down and say, 'that's enough.' Blue was in the first throws of passion and now was not the time. He looked in the mirror, rolled the legs up as far as possible and studied the result.

'Nope.' He conceded defeat and put on the chino long strides. They would be hot, but Gloria had gone to so much trouble, he felt it was the least he could do.

Once attired he brushed his hair and deposited his hat on his head. *Not 'arf bad*, he thought looking at his refection in the mirror.

Gloria had left a small salad for his tea, before he went to the 'do'. She started her shift at 5:30. Blue sat at the table and picked at the salad. It had things in it he had never seen before. He toyed with it, then threw it in the bin. It was a rash moment. He found some scrap paper and covered his criminality, then against all the odds he did his dishes, wiped the sink over and hung up the tea towel. Domestication in wild animals sometimes takes years of work. Gloria had accomplished it with one afternoon delight and a cup of tea.

Wollopi's residents were out in force. Bill had put on raspberry cordial for the kids and they hung about on the steps of the Peninsular Bar & Grill getting drunk, while their parents were inside getting drunk.

Bluey opened the door and pushed his way to the bar.

'What the f...' Slim didn't get any further with is critique of Bluey's sartorial elegance when he copped a fly swat.

'Owww. WhaddIdo?' Slim slunk back to his bar stool.

Jocko had more sense and raised his eye brows and whistled. 'Looking sharp Blue.'

'Nah.' Blue hopped up on a bar stool and smiled at Gloria. She smiled back and the exchange wasn't lost on the rubberneckers. Jocko nudged Slim with his elbow and gave a low whistle.

'Never.'

'I'll take a bet on it.' Jocko said.

'Blue,'

'Yeah,'

'Are they flamingos on ya shirt there?'

'Flamin' what?'

'Flamingos, ya know, the birds.'

Blue looked at Gloria. 'Are they?'

She nodded.

'Told ya.' Jocko slapped his beer mat on the counter and said, 'Slim, mate, ya owe me a drink.'

As the fan in the ceiling tried to keep pace with the fug of humanity after a hot day, Bill and Gloria were flat out, and while Maylee was in the Ladies Lounge setting up the tables, Jeremy Swindon began to sweat.

He'd never been beyond the black stump and wondered at the hospitality of the crowd if it all went to hell – which was on the cards as anyone with connectivity will attest. If it can go wrong, it usually does. He looked at the biceps and triceps of some of the blokes. They looked like they cracked nuts in their elbows just for fun.

Jeremy knocked back his beer and tried to think calming thoughts. The satellite dish was up. The wires connected. The trial run was smooth and it was all systems go. He just hoped it would go at 7.05 when he pushed the button. It was going to be a tense moment. His standard line of,

'Well, that's never happened before,' might work at the shopping centre, but out the back of beyond he reckoned things could get ugly. His girlfriend had said she read on the internet that someone was branded for leaving a gate open.

'What happened?' Jeremy asked, thinking police investigation, litigation and compensation.

'Dunno, my internet went down so I couldn't read the rest of the story.'

'Jeremy Swindon paid for another beer and hoped to get out alive.

'So Jocko, I thought you was gonna be away. The big op an' all that?' Blue said.

'Yeah, all set and then they cancelled on me. Just like that.'

'True?'

'Yeah,' Jocko shrugged at Slims exclamation.

'I gotta wait, the Doc said and well I said, ok mate, I can wait.'

'Bloody hell.'

'It sounds like psychosomatic to me.' Jeremy said and as he watched Jocko take a breath he instantly regretted his words.

'I had psychosomatic once. Gave me merry hell I tell ya.' Jocko clutched at his back.

'Never.'

'Yeah, ya never want that. Doc said I had it bad, real bad.'

'True.' Slim was captivated.

'Bloody oath. Said it was a miracle I was even walkin' around.'

'Jeez.'

Jeremy Swindon rolled his eyes to the ceiling and gathered up his beer.

'Did I tell ya about the time I was …' Jocko began when Jeremy took a look at a seat as far away as possible from the bar and headed in the general direction. He was scooped up by Crispin and ushered to the booth, before his feet touched the ground.

'I found him at the bar.' Crispin said to Rupert who was holding the booth from interlopers.

'He's that internet fellow.'

'Sit.' Rupert patted the seat. Jeremy sat.

After introductions Jeremy felt he owed R & C a drink.

'Thanks.'

'Oh Jocko, he's harmless. Well almost.' Rupert patted Jeremy's hand. 'Crispin on the other hand is a devil.' Crispin blushed.

'So, what do you have for us tonight Jeremy Swindon?'

And Jeremy couldn't help himself. R & C were hairdressers and that said it all. They could wheedle every last personal detail from you before you had time to pick up a Woman's Weekly. And when you are feeling out of your comfort zone, in the middle of Woop Woop, and you have an aversion to being branded with a hot iron, it's easy to let it all out.

Crispin patted Jeremy's hand as he let it all out.

'Honey, don't worry.'

'But I don't even like needles.' Jeremy was getting jumpy as he looked at his smart watch. Some of the farmer types were getting rowdy. He wondered if they still had things like the lazy A ranch branding irons.

'Look, sweetie, this lot are all bluff. You can press your buttons and in three minutes it will be all over.' Rupert looked at the B & G crowd. They were sweating, drinking, and wilting in the heat.

'That's what I'm afraid of.' Jeremy desperately wanted another beer, but the bar was too close to Jocko.

'Relax.' Rupert went for drinks.

'I have an idea.' Crispin said and leaned in. Jeremy was all ears.

Bill and Maylee stood on seats at the bar and Bill whistled through the gap where his teeth should have been.

'Listen up.'

The Bar and Grill quietened down and all eyes looked to Bill.

'We gonna get connected tonight.' Bill stated the obvious.

The crowd sweated a bit more as they listened.

'Where's the in-ter-net bloke?'

'Here.' Jeremy was hoiked to his feet, beer in hand. The crowd cheered and went back to drinking. It was getting mighty hot.

Jeremy staggered to the computer at the far end of the bar and plugged in his smart phone. He plinked and plunked his keypad and then gave the thumbs up to Bill.

'Oi.' Bill grabbed the crowd's attention.

'We're getting connected now.'

The crowd counted down the seconds as if it was New Year's Eve.

Jeremy pressed the button and all eyes looked to the big screen.

There for all to see were pictures of the patrons of the Bar and Grill and Wollopi.

Brenda was snogging Chad, who was married to Eve at the time. Garth was taking a slash behind Norm's car, Maylee was eating a sausage while Bill looked on, Wes was dead drunk sleeping on a car bonnet, Slim was getting slapped with a flyswat, Gloria was hanging over the bar, and as the pictures scrolled they showed the townfolk in all their glory. Crispin winked at Rupert and Jeremy? Well, he was manhandled to the shoulders of the patrons, just missing the ceiling fan and paraded around the room as if he had single handedly won Wollopi's nomination for hosting the Olympics.

The beer flowed, Jeremy got plastered and anything after 7:30 was just a blur. Jocko fell off his bar stool and hurt his psychosomatic, Slim passed out somewhere between the dunny and jukebox and Bluey drank 6 schooners and fell in love.

'Gloria,' Bluey said as she gave him a rum.
'Yes.'

'Gloria,' Bluey said and leaned on the bar to slup another rum down his neck.

'Yes?'

'You're a good sort.'

'Thanks.'

'You're the best sort. Ya bloody t'riffic.'

'Thanks.' Gloria poured one more rum for Blue.

'Ya the best.'

'Oh, Blue.'

'I think I love ya.'

'Oh, Blue.'

'I think I love ya and I think I wanna marry ya.'

'Oh, Blue.' Gloria kissed the man of her dreams and corked the bottle.

'Did ya hear that.' Blue was feeling expansive. 6 schooners will do that.

'What?' Bill asked as he popped another spring roll in his mouth.

'I'm gonna marry Gloria.'

'Never.' Bill said.

'Yep.' Blue was also feeling the man of the hour.

'Ya hear that. Bluey here's gone an' asked Gloria to marry him.'

The crowd cheered. 'Drinks, drinks,' they chanted. Bill had had one too many spring rolls, which make a man extra thirsty, which necessitates a few beers, quite a few beers. He looked for his wife. She was in the Ladies Lounge and so he did something he hoped his wouldn't regret.

'The drinks are on the house.' He didn't need to say it twice. The crush was akin to the old 6 o'clock swill.

Bluey was toasted. Gloria was toasted. Slim was toast. They had their photos taken. They were shoved together and pulled apart and shoved together again. They were slapped on the back. And when it was ascertained that Gloria hadn't said yes, Bill asked for quiet.

'G'on. Blue ask her again.'

'What?' Blue had upped the mark to 8 schooners and three chasers, Rum, Scotch and Vodka, and wasn't clear on the question never mind the answer.

'G'on. Ask her again.'

'What?'

'Oh, Blue, Yes. Yes. Yes.' Gloria said and gave him a kiss.

The bar erupted once again with 'Drinks, drinks.' Bill caught his wife's eye and giggled.

'Nah,' Bill said.

That small word deadened the atmosphere like a match in a blimp. Within 3 minutes the crowd had thinned and they finally found Slim on the floor.

Gloria's place at Manooka Drive was just a stone's throw from The Bar & Grill as the crow flies, but by car you need to traverse the old Whetstone bridge about two clicks west, then double back on the other side of Wollopi Creek.

Gloria bundled her fiancé into her car and headed for home. They got as far as the bridge and suddenly the fresh air was toxic. Blue always thought fresh air was the problem with the world. He yelled to stop the car and hurled himself out to the bridge rail and chucked up. Gloria waited, she wasn't about to let Bluey get away.

'You a'right?'

'Yeeeeeaaaahh.' Blue gurgled.

'You want a mint?' Gloria fossicked around in the glove compartment and came up with a tic-tac. 'Mint?' She offered.

Blue sat in the car and popped the mint in his mouth.

'I spewed me guts.' He took the mint. 'Ta.'

'Not a problem.' Gloria leaned over and closed the door. 'Be home soon Luv.'

'Glooooooqqqaaaaah.' Bluey thought he might have left his tongue back on the bridge.

'Oh, Blue.' Gloria took the noise as a compliment.

She pulled up at her house, 'Let's get you inside.'

'I lubbbbbb ya.'

'I know honey, I know.' Gloria pulled her man to the lounge room and sat him down. 'Sit here, I won't be a sec.' She went to the kitchen … as I said, she was of Polish decent. All ills, ails, and incoherence could be fixed with food. Sauerkraut is practically a wonder drug.

Bluey slid down to the floor and made himself comfortably unconscious.

He woke up to the smell of toast and sausage. It's amazing how hungry one can get when you've been to the pub.

He sat up and focussed on Gloria bending down offering him some supper.

'It'll do you good Blue.' She put a fork in his hand and he dutifully ate his way to nearly sober.

It was way past midnight when they had finished the cake and Gloria snuggled up to her newly intended.

'So Bluey.' Gloria curled herself around Bluey and twirled his few remaining hairs around her little finger.

'Yeah.' Blue burped.

'Now we engaged an' everything.'

'Yeah.' Blue was feeling mellow and the whole world was bathed in the light of Polish sausage.

'Well, I was thinking an' everything that I can't just keep calling you Bluey for the rest of our lives.'

'Nah. S'allright.'

'Really. I should know your real name.'

'Nah. S'o.k.'

'What did ya dad call ya?' Gloria twiddled Blue's earlobe.

'Cunt.'

Gloria had heard worse at the Bar & Grill. She slapped him playfully. 'Oh Bluey.' She kissed him and while he was thus occupied she pulled his wallet out of his back pocket and reached for his driver's licence.

'Oh, Blue.' Gloria read the name. 'Meredith Francis Gaylore.'

'Yeah.' Bluey rested his head on Gloria's ample bosom.

'Mrs Gaylore.'

'That's me mum.'

Gloria mused on the name. 'Gloria Gaylore,' It had a musical ring to it.

What was, at midnight, a small affair, soon turned into a rather large affair by 10am the next day. Bluey was oblivious to the workings of the town's grapevine, Gloria was the one with the fertilizer.

By 11am the news was heard, remarked upon, debated, and disseminated. Once it hit the hairdressers there was no need to put something in the local rag. Everyone who was a ratepayer knew that Gloria Gerkoff was marrying Meredith Gaylore. Most agreed it could only be a good thing to get rid of that Polish surname, pronounced as it was in Wollopi with the G as in Geoffrey.

Bluey woke to Ralph sleeping on his chest. He patted his best mate and then, like a man who has realizes too late they signed up for the pledge rather than a meat tray, he sat bolt upright and uttered the words, most men utter at one time or another in their lives,

'What have I done.'

Ralph looked suitably unimpressed. He roamed around in a circle twice and settled down on the end of the bed.

Bluey burped and the whole sorry event came back to haunt him with Polish sausage aftertaste.

'Ralph, mate.'

Ralph scratched his new collar. Blue saw the flamin' flamingo shirt on the floor. He felt sick. He felt duped. He felt in his pocket for his car keys. It then dawned on him he didn't have any pockets. In fact, he was in the nuddy.

'Mate.'

There is just so much a man can do in the face of mounting evidence. Blue lay down and put his hands behind his head and contemplated a life of Polish Pierogi and his and hers matching bath towels.

There was a note on the kitchen table. Gloria had provided lunch. She indicated he should do his dishes. She advised him that she would wash his clothes in the evening and lastly he was instructed to ring his family.

'Bloody Nora.' Blue scratched the back of his neck and sat down.

They were all reasonable requests, and to be fair Gloria was only trying to domesticate him by degrees, but to Blue it felt a little rushed. The first flush of love will only get you so far in the scheme of things.

He opened the fridge and found something edible. Ralph nosed around and was rewarded with a sausage. Bluey knew the perils of Ralph and sausages, but he was beginning to get the 'what the heck' feeling.

What he needed, he felt, was a bit of blokey, bloke stuff. The pub came to mind.

'She hasn't got me yet,' he said to Ralph and soon he was in his shorts and singlet and heading for the B & G.

He stepped through the door and Gloria smiled at him and waved.

'Bluey smiled back,' he couldn't help himself; every time he saw Gloria she stirred something within him, probably his testostolones, as Jocko would say.

'G'day mate.' Slim slapped Bluey on the back.

'G'day.'

'How's it goin'?' Jocko asked and winked.

'Bonzer.' Blue hopped up on a bar stool and Gloria poured him a beer.

'There ya go luv.' She leaned on the bar and smiled.

Bluey smiled back, like the man who smiles for the camera before he is hanged.

Jocko and Slim watched with morbid fascination. They should have been watching the races on the internet, except a crow had picked off a vital component at first light and Jeremy Swindon had said it would now take a week for the spare part as he hastily made for his car. The dust hardly had time to settle and Mr Swindon was about 50 click away and vowing to never go further than the supermarket in the near future. The tale he would relate in the staff room after the team hug and bonding session would be full of derring-do and he was lucky to get out alive.

Bluey was feeling a little of the same. He swallowed his beer and it left a bitter taste of disappointment. After a lifetime of drinking Bluey thought he knew his limits. He thought he had control of his urges to love the whole world and everyone in it. He thought he could handle 8 schooners and a few chasers.

'Bluey,' Gloria leaned over the bar and her assets put all Bluey's controls on high alert.

'Yeah,' he said and then added, 'luv.'

'Did you ring?'

'Who?'

'Oh, Blue. Stop joking.' Gloria gave him a teasing thump on the arm.

'Oh, yeah. Um, well I forgot the number see, and I was gonna say how about you do it. You're good at that sort of thing like, and um, I just thought you could ya know…'

'Oh, Blue.' Gloria leaned over a little further and Slim missed his mouth. His beer cascaded down his shirt front.

'Shit.'

Gloria pulled the fly swat and threatened him.

'WhaddaIdo?'

'Just watch it.'

'A'right.'

Bluey was passed the phone and it was all over red rover.

Once you announce to your sister that you intend to get hitched, you might as well buy a ring.

He hung up and scratched the back of his head.

'Whadshesay?' Slim asked.

'She said as soon as we set a date, she's comin' up.'

'She bringin' that I-ran fella?'

Bluey could only shrug.

'Ya settin' a date then?' Slim kept up the interrogation.

Bluey bit his lip. 'Dunno.'

'Ya fixin' to hire the whole box and dice Blue?'

'Willyajustshut it?' Jocko said, 'Can't ya see the man's thinkin'.'

Gloria waved the swat around and Slim cowered.

'WhadIsay?'

'We're getting married in three weeks, if you must know.'

Bluey looked at Slim and shrugged and gave one of those sheepish grins that sheep give when they realise they only have a small brain capacity.

'A bit of a do.' Jocko said.

'Yeah, a bit of a do.' Bluey looked to Gloria for confirmation.

'That's right. A bit of a do.'

And that's how it happened.

A do requires planning. A do requires more than a bit of cash behind the bar. Lucky for Bluey, Gloria had the organisational skills of a mother of six on shift work. She liaised with Maylee, she conferred with the local dressmaker and she hired a suit for Bluey. All was going well when Crispin and Rupert came in on the dot of 1:15.

'Oh there she is, the blushing bride.' Rupert was caught up in the moment.

'Tell all Gloria,' Crispin hopped up on a bar stool and put a twenty on the bar. 'Have one on us darling.'

Blue, Jocko and Slim watched as Gloria poured herself a malt whiskey, dropped a cube of ice and slugged back the shot in one.

'Thanks.'

'Not a prob.' Crispin smiled.

'So, darling, are you having a do?'

'Hmmm.'

'Lovely. And who's doing your …um….hair?' Crispin waved his hands about trying to describe the very particular hair style Gloria had cultivated over the decades.

'Me?' she squeaked.

'Oh, no. On the house. We'd love to, wouldn't we Rupert?'

'Absobloodylutely.' Rupert blew an air kiss. He looked over to Blue.

'And your man?'

220

'Me?' Blue squeaked.

'Of course you dearie.'

'Nah, she's right.' Blue felt for his hat to make sure it was on tight.

'Oh, honestly,' Rupert patted Blue's hand. 'Bring him along Gloria, and we'll see what we can do.' There was a large wave of a hand and R & C retired to their booth.

'Ya goin' to the shearin' shed Blue?' Slim asked with a smirk on his face.

'He's going.' Gloria wiped the bar and shot the love of her life a look that a blind man could see in the dark.

'Um… Yeah.'

'Oh, Gloria,' Rupert waved in the direction of the bar.

Gloria walked over.

'Who's catering dear?'

'Maylee?' Gloria suggested.

'I know just what you're thinking.' Rupert said to Crispin.

'Really?'

Rupert smirked. 'Giles Malthorpe.'

'Oh, you.' Crispin slapped Rupert's hand. 'You know me so well.'

Giles Malthorpe was a chef, with a helicopter, a house on Sydney Harbour and his own T.V. show. He was also a friend of Crispin's from way back. They kept in touch.

'Honey, can you tell Maylee we'll do what we can for catering.'

'Hang on a sec.' Gloria called upstairs on the intercom.

Jocko, Slim and Bluey hung on the conversation like they were counter intelligence for the rival CWA.

There was a thumbs up in the direction of the booth.

'Well, isn't this going to be fun.' R & C gave each other a high five.

'Ya got a best man yet Blue?' Slim's eyebrows shot up.

'Nah.' Bluey missed the nuance.

'Ya want one?'

'Dunno,' but as he said it the thought occurred to him.

'Yeah. I guess so.'

'Thanks mate. I won't let ya down. We'll have a real beaut bucks night. Strippers and the lot.' Slim was on a roll.

'I reckon I'll ask me mate, Abdul.'

'Huh?'

'Yeah,' Blue said as the thought took shape. 'Yep, that's it. I'm gonna ask him. He's a good bloke.'

Sylvia Rentree sat at Gwen's kitchen table and fiddled with the crumbs on her plate.

'He's really looking forward to it Sylvia.' Gwen poured another cup of tea and pushed the milk Syliva's way.

'We're not s'posed to fraternise with clients.'

'He's not a client Sylvia, he's Hakim. He likes you. He wants you to come to a mate's wedding. C'on, it'll be fun.' Ms Rentree sipped her tea and let out a long languid sigh.

'You like him don't cha?'

'Well,'

'Knew it.' Gwen gathered the crumbs from her frangipani pie in her hand and tossed them in the sink.

'And?'

'And, well … I feel as a feminist that I should not take an invitation by a man as the downgrading of my standing as a human being and …'

'Oh, give it a rest Sylvia. Feminism, shamanism.' Gwen put it into perspective. 'I'm askin' ya, alright.'

'You?'

'Yeah, Me. The downtrodden woman who washes men's clothes, cooks their tea and buy's their underwear.'

'Ok then.' Sylvia took another slice of pie, sometimes called humble pie.

To move eleven people, you need something called a people mover – obviously.

Darren and his intended drove up in a big mini-van – an oxymoron if ever there was one – and honked the horn.

Sylvia shaded her eyes and stepped from the verandah. She'd become a platinum blonde for the occasion and her hair positively glowed in the sun.

Agnes was helped down the steps by Lance, and Hakim took her overnight bag to the boot of the van.

Next were the two kids, Skyla and Bob rounded up by their father, Rod.

Gwen and Rayleen came out with bags, food, blankets, thermoses of coffee, cordial and Beaut, the dog.

Darren helped load enough stuff to survive the outback until the nuclear holocaust.

'Ya sure we need this mum?' He picked up a mega, super, jumbo cube of toilet paper.

'Ya never know out there. It's way beyond the black stump and well…ya just never know.'

In it went in no particular order.

'We got air-con dad.' Bob was excited beyond measure.

'I'm gonna be the bridesmaid for uncle Bluey,' Skyla had deposited herself next to Sylvia and started to talk. It would be a marathon effort as Skyla was one of those kids that doesn't know how to shut up. For Sylvia it would be a salutary lesson in the what goes on in the real world where girls want to be princesses and bridesmaids and boys want to cut the eyes off snails and hammer ants.

'Did someone turn the tele on?' Agnes asked. The family had invested in a 7 day recorder bought off the local Buy, swap and sell.

'Yeah, all good mum.' Gwen sat down and wiped the sweat from her brow. She turned around and surveyed the seating, counting heads.

'A'right Gwen?' Lance was sitting at the back with Rod and Hakim.

'S'a'right luv.'

At that pronouncement Darren started the van and they were off to Wollopi; with toilet stops, snack stops, stretch ya legs stops and 'oooo will ya look at that' stops' (for someone had brought Bob a disposable camera) it was going to take all day and then some.

Darren's intended pulled out a neck pillow, blew it up, fetched a battery fan and clipped it to the seat in front and went to sleep.

Gwen pulled a face and rolled her eyes at Rayleen. They heard the familiar pfft of a ring pull from the back of the bus.

'Just the one luv,' Lance said, as his wife turned to give him a withering stare.

Hakim and Rod pulled a coldie from the esky and sat back.

'Bloody livin' init?'

'Bloody rippa,' Hakim said.

'Bloody t'riffic.' Rod concurred.

'Mum, dad's swearing,' Bob said and took a photo.

About three hours in, after Sylvia had heard all about how unicorns are made and why fairy dust is so expensive, Agnes let out a yell and everyone jumped awake.

'What?'

'Bloody hell?'

'Mum?'

Agnes punched the T.V weekly and let out a howl. 'I'm missing the last episode of Block Fever.'

There was a collective sigh of relief. 'We got it covered mum,' Lance said.

'Oh, good boy.' Agnes went back to her T.V. guide.

'She likes ya, ya know that don't cha?' Rod jabbed Hakim in the ribs.

'Agnes?'

'Nah, the sheila, Sylvia.'

'I am knowing this.' Hakim grinned. 'She's a bloody rippa.'

'Ya pretty damn good with the lingo now.' Rod said.

'Yeah, pretty damn good.'

'Ya still goin' to ya school an' all that?'

'Yes thank you very much for asking,' he said with a posh accent.

'They teach ya that did they?'

'I am learning English.'

'Nah, ya don't wanna learn English. Ya wanna learn our lingo Hakim. The real Ozzie lingo.' Rod said.

'I am learning at work.'

'He's right there ya know. I heard 'im talking to his boss.

'Reg West.' Hakim offered.

'He's an alright bloke, Westie.'

'Look, wanna get ahead of the game?'

'Game?'

'Wanna get it straight from the horse's mouth.'

Hakim nodded and frowned.

'Right.' Rod took a deep breath and began.

'First,' he said,

'Sheila is a girl, the good sort.' He pointed to Sylvia.

The list began.

'Smoko,' Lance added.

'I know smoko.' Hakim said.

Drongo is an idiot

Ocker is an Australian

Noggin' that's your head.

Chinwag is having a natter. A talk.

Iffy is a bit sus, a bit suspicious.

Gander is giving something a look.

Nuddy is in the altogether. In the nude.

'Arvo,' Bob said.

'Good one son.' Rod gave his son a high five. 'That's the afternoon.

'Furphy,' Agnes added.

'That's a lie,' Rod said.

'So ya could say sommit like, I was havin' a chinwag with a sheila in the arvo and a drongo who was a bit iffy and not much in the noggin took a gander at us and ran around in the nuddy.'

Bob thought the whole thing hilarious. 'I think this is a furphy.' Hakim said and that topped it off.

Darren pulled the bus into a servo and the troops gathered at the toilet.

'Where's Darren's intended?' Gwen asked Agnes.

'Sleeping.' Agnes went into the loo after Skyla.

Inside the servo Darren lined up with Lance to pay, when they caught the conversation in front. The blokes were outback types, rough around the edges.

'Look I'm tellin' ya, forget Brockie.'

'He was great thou'.'

'Yeah, but forget it. Let's drink some piss and root some of them dirty sluts.'

Lance looked at his son. Darren looked at his mother collecting life saver lollies for the kids. They wouldn't save her from the outback. She rolled her eyes.

'I don't think we're in Kansas anymore,' Darren whispered to his dad.

'Bloody oath.' Lance grinned.

Sylvia wandered out onto the verandah and stretched to scratch Beaut's head. The dog rolled over for the $10 special.

'It is a good trip. Bloody rippa.' Hakim patted Beaut's belly.

'Not bad.' Sylvia said and sat down on a rubbish bin, one of the anomalies of travel is that you sit all day and when you have a break, all you want to do is sit.

'Hakim?'

'Yes?'

'I'm glad you asked me.'

'I'm glad too.' Hakim said. 'I need to ask you a question?'

'Yes.'

'What is a best man?'

'Well,' Sylvia tried to frame her answer without the usual diatribe of outdated, matrimonial constructs made to subjugate women and devalue half the population with machoistic propaganda and cultural concepts. It wasn't easy.

'It's the man who helps the groom prepare for his wedding. His best friend.'

'His best friend.'

'Yep.'

'I am Bluey's best friend?'

'I reckon so.' Sylvia nodded.

'He is my best friend.'

'Yep.'

'He is my best man.'

'Well, it only happens when you get married, but yep, that's about it.'

'Thank you.' Hakim went into the servo and came back with two iceblocks. He handed the fast melting treat to Sylvia and they ate them as quick as their front teeth would allow.

'Thanks Hakim.'

Darren tooted the horn and the family filed back into the van past sleeping beauty.

Sylvia grabbed Hakim and pulled him into the seat next to her. Skyla had to sit with great grandma, Rod was seated with his wife and Gwen had control of Bob and Lance was left with Beaut, the dog.

'And you know that unicorns are the colour of the rainbow granny.' Sylvia smiled, she'd managed to dodge that particular rainbow bullet.

'You are nice when you smile.'

'Oh, Hakim.' Sylvia said and twirled his hair around her little finger.

At the top of Plinthe Hill the family stopped and admired the view. Bob had used all his photos taking pictures of the back of his father's head, so they all stared into the distance in silence.

'That's Australia Hakim,' Sylvia pointed to the wide brown land.

'Better than New Bloody Zealand.'

'Yeah, better, much better,' Rod said and put his hand on Bob's shoulders.

'It's a long way isn't it Mum?' Skyla said.

'Yep.' Rayleen shoed a fly away from her daughter's face.

'Make's ya feel small.' Agnes shaded her eyes and squinted into the distance.

'And a bit proud too.' Gwen added.

'Yeah.' Lance swatted a fly.

'It kinda goes on forever.' Darren said as he spat a fly out.

'C'on.'

They piled back into the van and the air-con was cranked over to full. Darren's intended slept on.

'She missed Plinthe Hill,' Agnes said.

'Yeah.' Darren shrugged and put the van in gear.

At Mackley's Crossing Hakim stood up and told Darren to stop.

He looked at his fellow passengers and announced.

'Here I met Bluey.'

They all jumbled out of the van and stood about in the sun, swatting flies.

'It was here.' Hakim stood on the very spot.

'Here?' Rayleen pointed.

'Yep.'

'Right here?' Gwen asked.

'Yep.

'Jeez.' Lance looked at the desolate spot. 'Ya was way out here eh?'

'Too right.' Hakim grabbed Sylvia's hand and stood on the road.

'I am very happy because of you.'

'Oh, Hakim.' Sylvia shuffled the red dirt with the toe of her sandal and waved a fly away from her nostril. 'That's the nicest thing anyone has said to me.' Beaut raced about on the road sniffing and snapping at flies.

Gwen nudged Lance and gave him a wink.

'Mum, I swallowed a fly.' Bob tried to spit.

'Then you won't want tea.' Rayleen said.

'Oh, Mum.' Bob's plaintive cry roused the group and they retreated to the bug free zone of the van.

Three hours from the crossing was Wollopi.

'Are we there yet?'

'Are we there yet?'

It was repeated nine times; Darren's intended was still asleep.

'Does she even have a bladder?' Rayleen asked Gwen. 'I dunno luv.'

Darren drove with dogged determination, Beaut sitting beside him, and as the sun set they slowed for the main street of Wollopi.

There wasn't a lot to see at 8:15pm.

The one bright light was the Peninsular Bar & Grill.

'That's it,' Lance pointed to the neon sign. He could almost taste a cold one.

Darren swung into the car park and cut the engine.

His intended yawned and stretched.

'She's alive then?' Agnes said.

'Oh, we've arrived.' Her specialty was stating the obvious.

Lance was first over the threshold. He spied Bluey sitting at the Bar, 'G'day Bluey.'

'Jeez' Bluey cracked a smile as the rest of the crew filed into the bar, upping the clientele by 200%.

'Are we in a pub Mum?' Skyla asked.

'Yes luv.'

'Is this where Dad lives?'

'No luv.'

'But you said he lives in the pub.'

Rayleen looked at her husband and shrugged and gave a little giggle.

'Kids, they say the darnest things.'

'Bluey,' Agnes hugged her son and planted a kiss on his cheek.

'It's me mum.' Blue said to Jocko and Slim.

'G'day.' Slim smiled and raised his beer.

'Howdy,' Jocko held out his hand.

Agnes shook the hand and then wiped her palm on her tracksuit pants.

'Bluey,' Rod slapped Blue on the back.

'Hi Uncle Bluey,' Darren pushed to the front, 'This is my intended.'

'Pleased to meet ya.' Blue stuck out his hand.

Gwen came to the front and planted a kiss on her brother's cheek. 'Ya a dark one eh. Getting married an' all that. Who'd of thought.' She stood back, 'This is Gloria is it.'

'Yeah,' Bluey rubbed the back of his neck and smiled at Gloria who had been watching the whole parade of relatives. They descended on Gloria, shaking hands, talking.

'And your family coming too Gloria?'

'No. Me mum and dad passed some time ago. You know how it is. Just me.'

'Oh.' Gwen frowned. 'Well, we're family now and that's all there is to it.' The matriarch had spoken. Bluey winked at the love of his life. She was family now.

'And then Bluey saw Hakim.'

'Mate,' Blue pushed past his nearest and dearest and strode over to Hakim.

'Abdul, bloody Abdul.'

'Hakim.'

And they gave each other a manly hug with much back slapping, and arm punching.

'Good to see ya.'

'Good to see ya.'

'Mate.'

'Mate.'

'I am happy.'

'Yeah.'

'I have a special friend.' Hakim grabbed Sylvia and thrust her forward.

'Sylvia. She is my friend and I have a dog.'

'She's his sheila.' Gwen came into the conversation.

'Ya shittin' me.'

'Nope.'

'Bloody Nora.'

'Pleased to meet you Bluey.' Sylvia gave Blue a small continental peck on the cheek.

'Jeez.' Slim and Jocko watched the whole thing.

'He's from one of them Arabie countries inhe?'

'Yeah.'

'Any mate of Bluey's is a'right by me.' Jocko said.

'Me too.' Slim sipped his beer.

With the formalities over Gwen pulled Gloria aside and asked where Blue had booked them for accommodation.

'We've been at it all day and we're buggered.'

'Bluey?' Gloria called the love of her life over with a voice of a headmistress who has found a cigarette in the girl's toilets.

'Yeah, luv?' Blue hid behind his schooner of beer.

Accommodating eleven people and a dog at short notice is not an easy task. Gloria made a few phone calls, reminded a few people what they owed on their tab, jolted a few memories of who was with who and when, and only then, when she had exhausted every possibility, she rang R & C. They occupied the biggest house, which was a converted warehouse and had, it was rumoured, three bathrooms and a jacuzzi.

Rod let out a whistle as he stepped into the front room of R & C home.

'It's swish init.' Agnes looked at the modern décor and recognised a few hints from her favourite show.

Rayleen's eyes popped as she saw the spacious kitchen with all mod cons. She nudged her mum and they swooned over the magnetic knife block and the copper pots hanging over the stove.

'Welcome, come in, come in.' Rupert pulled his smoking jacket a little closer over his chest and waved the crowd of gawkers into the sunken lounge.

Bluey smiled and tilted his hat back on his head, 'It's bloody nice of ya to do this for me family an' all that.'

'Not a prob, always glad to lend a hand, aren't we Ruppee,' Crispin said.

'Now, sit down everyone.'

Hakim stood about as all the chairs were taken,

'Sit on the poof.' Gwen said pointing to the ottoman in the corner.

'Oh, honey, not yet.' Rupert blushed and nudged Crispin.

'He's rather naughty I'm afraid.' Crispin said. Rod stifled a grin. Anyone for coffee?' Crispin added.

The crowd sat still and straight everyone on their best behaviour as they sipped expresso. Bob had crashed on the floor, and Skyla wasn't far behind, leaning on her mother with that dead weight look in her eyes.

'So,' Rupert clapped his hands, 'what do we need in the way of beds and such?'

'Well,' Gwen looked over the travel weary family and explained the sleeping arrangements of couples when she looked at Hakim and Sylvia and raised her eyebrows

'I'll just kip with Agnes, Sylvia said pre-empting any discussion.

It was a jumble of bags, toilet paper, themos flasks and eskies but by eleven o'clock everyone was in their allotted rooms, on camp beds, on blow up beds and futons.

'What'd he call it dearie?'

'It's a futon, Mrs Gaylore.' Sylvia lay down and looked at the ceiling by the light of the moon and thought of a hair dye to match a wedding cake.

'Do you think they're gay Lance.' Gwen held her husband's hand.

'I reckon, ya get a gander at their slippers. Poofs if ever I seen one.' Obviously, Lance knew a thing or two about the night time attire of homosexuals. Don't ask me how.

'Did you see that kitchen Rod?'

'Yeah.'

'Do you think we could do something like that?'

'Nah.'

'Please.'

'You awake darling?'

Darren's intended nodded off the minute her head hit the pillow.

'Uncle Darren, did you know unicorns are the colour of the rainbow.'

'Mr Hakim?'
'Yes.'
'I'm awake now.' Bob had got his second wind.

And over at Manooka Drive Gloria was washing the dishes from supper and said,
'I'm gonna ask your mum why she chose Meredith.'
'I know that.' Bluey wiped the last plate.
'Well?'
'She's crazy on the movies. There was a film star bloke. Meredith someone or other.'
'And Francis?'
'Don't ask.'
'Oh, come on Bluey. I'm your fiancé, you can tell me.'
'Nah.'
'Bluey.' Gloria pecked him on the cheek.
'A good win at 20 to 1 in the 1:30 at Mooney Ponds. Me dad had a sense of humour.'
'Where's ya dad now?'
'Died laughin' I guess.' Bluey folded the tea-towel and hung it up on the rail.

And as the lights went out Gloria realised she was thirsty. When it's been a long time between drinks, a person can get a mighty thirsty.

The family and crew gathered at the breakfast table and admired the skill of R &n C in the kitchen. Rayleen was agog; that word didn't happen often in Wollopi, I assure you.

'Are you two, umm,' Lance started when he was kicked under the table by his wife.

'I was just askin' if they were, you know, like, you know, professionals or someit?' Lance rubbed his shin.

'Professionals?'

'Yeah.'

'We're hairdressers luvvie.'

'Oh.' Lance's suspicions were confirmed, put in a box and filed away. 'Hairdressers eh?'

Rayleen touched her hair. The most she got around to in the way of style was pulling it behind her ears. Everyone looked to Lance and his comb-over.

'What?'

'Nothing darling, nothing at all.' Rupert rolled his tongue over his teeth and frowned in that hang dog way that a vet frowns when telling the owner there is nothing he can do.

'We're doing the wedding hair.' Crispin said gaily.

'Oh.' Gwen nodded touching her birds nest.

'Really,' Sylvia bit her top lip.

'Fancy.' Rayleen shrugged and giggled.

'Oh, what the heck.' Crispin slapped his hands on the counter. 'We'll just throw ourselves into the whole shebang and to hell with the consequences.'

'We've got a day up our sleeve, who's first.' Rupert said. Gwen, Rayleen and Sylvia grinned at one another. Darren's intended was still asleep.

'Do you have a tele?' Agnes asked. 'I like the tele.'

'Of course you do.' Rupert showed Agnes to the media room. It sported a 71-inch screen on the wall with surround sound. 'It's only satellite I'm afraid.' Agnes nearly choked on her warm croissant with English marmalade.

By the time the women had had the once over, R & C knew all about the family, Agnes's operation, the ages and stages of the kids, the habits of the men, good and bad and Bluey's love life as far back as Gwen could recollect. Rupert and Crispin did their best with what they had and the women were suitably impressed. Sylvia looked at herself in the mirror. She had been transformed from Bolshevik feminist to an attractive 24 year old platinum bomb shell.

'Honey, you'll kill the competition.' Rupert swung her around in the chair and swooned.

'How do you do it?' Rayleen asked as she swung her new hair about her neck.

Rupert looked at Crispin. Crispin looked at Rupert.

'We were hairdressers to the stars, but don't tell will you.'

'Stars?' Gwen asked patting her hair and looking in the mirror.

'Oh, only television honey, but the secrets we could tell.' Rupert jabbed Crispin in the ribs with a hairdryer and they laughed.

'Now, I think…' Rupert tapped his lips with the end of a comb, 'icecream.'

'Oh, yes. I'ts got to be icecream.

'The girls just died right there in the hairdressing salon. It was too good to be true.

The men regrouped for the stag night.

For those who are lacking an education, a stag night is the one night where men can let their hair down, if they have any, that is.

It is the last night of bachelorhood for the groom and his mate's want to make it a memorable one. That no man ever remembers his stag night is neither here nor there. He must have had a blast, because either he didn't end up in hospital or he did end up in hospital.

Rod, Lance, Hakim and Darren *regrouped* at the Peninsular Bar & Grill.

Gloria was taking the afternoon off and Bill lounged over the bar listening to Jocko.

'So I said to the bloke, Wally I said, if ya want a dentist I'm ya man. I pulled me tooth out with a pair of multigrips once, when I was in the army.'

'Strewth.' Slim ran his tongue over the last of his teeth in his head.

'Yeah, piece of cake.' Jocko looked at the four new drinkers and smiled. They couldn't help but look at the gap between his front teeth and his molars. The gap was enough for a jack hammer.

'You blokes drinkin''

'You bet.' Lance hopped up on a bar stool and his hair took a minute to catch up.

'Lookin' sharp.' Jocko said and took a drink to hide his smirk.

'You hear for Blue then?' Slim wasn't the sharpest tool in the shed.

'Yeah, ya drongo, they're here for the do.' Jocko looked at Hakim. 'He's the best man.'

'I am the best man.' Hakim said and stood tall.

'A'right. A'right.' Slim rolled his eyes. 'I can't be remembering everyone.'

'Four's your limit.' Jocko put his empty glass on the bar and Bill gave him another.

'So mate, what ya got planned?' Slim asked. 'Strippers, pole dancers an' stuff.'

Darren looked at the bar, Slim, Jocko and Bill. He wondered if they even had a balloon in the place; he was sure they wouldn't have the telephone number of a stripper or pole dancer.

'Nah,' he said.

'Just some drinks I reckon.' Lance took his new schooner and supped.

'Ow.' Slim slunk back to his bar stool.

'Yeah, that's about it.' Rod handed his empty over and Bill filled it.

'I am the best friend.' Hakim finished his beer and another was pulled.

And so the regrouping continued into the late afternoon. It was after some considerable thought and a rather long story about directional boring that someone had the idea that Bluey should be in attendance. After all, it was his stag night. The thought was passed around, talked about, discussed and debated. No-one thought to go and fetch him.

About 7ish there was a phone call and Bill passed the message along. They were wanted, at home, NOW. It was a call that could not be ignored.

The party broke up and headed home. Everyone agreed it was a good night.

'Bloody rippa,' Hakim staggered along the main street.

'You said it,' Darren slapped him on the back and tripped over a blade of grass.

'Bloody t'riffic.' Rod burped.

'Yahppffblosojt4p2'jj=.' Lance just couldn't get anything past his tongue that made sense.

About 8pm Bluey sailed through the door of the B & G and sat at the bar.

'G'day mate.' Jocko smiled.

'Howdy.' Slim lifted his beer in greeting.

Blue had one or two. He waited. He looked at the Elvis clock on the wall. By 9:30 he'd had enough. Nerves can make a man go off his tucker. Stress can see a bloke give up drinking or take it up. Bluey tried both. He put his money in his pocket and left the B & G and walked home.

At least Gloria would be waiting with open arms, and a plate of something she just whipped up. He convinced himself he was a lucky man.

And he was.

Hair, makeup, lights, camera, action. It was all go in Wollopi the day of the wedding. Gloria was up at the crack of dawn for her facial and hair. She buzzed over to the salon and let R & C work their magic. They needed more than a magic wand to tame the beast of a hairstyle.

Bluey read the paper and ate his birdseed with natural yogurt. If you put enough sugar on it, it was edible. Love will do that to a man. He picked up the note left by Gloria.

Go to Goldstein at 10 for your suit. He had an hour up his sleeve so put on the clothes she had left out for him and wandered over to Rupert and Crispin's home. He whistled up Ralph.

The front door was open and he could hear voices.

'Hello.'

'Bluey,' Rod came to the door and ushered him in. Ralph poked his head inside and then trotted off to the garden.

'We're trying to get Bob into something other than shorts and t-shirt. He's kicking up a stink.

'Nah, it's kinda informal Gloria said. She'll be right.'

'Thanks.' Rod backtracked to the bedroom with the news.

Hakim came out of the kitchen and the men looked at one another.

Bluey had a polo shirt on with a GT stripe down the left side. Gloria had picked it out.

Hakim had a polo shirt on with a GT stripe down the right side. Sylvia had picked it out.

'Mate.'

'Mate.'

They stood open-mouthed looking at each other much like the salmon look at the next waterfall and think, I can't help myself. It's the call of the wild, or maybe the half-price sale at Goldstein's in the main street.

'Wanna come to get me suit?'

'Sure.' Hakim picked up his hat and followed Bluey out. They picked up Beaut on the way out.

'I am proud to be your best man.'

'Thanks.' Bluey took the lead and they walked to the haberdashery/drapers/shoe shop and clothing store, Ralph and Beaut managing to stop at every corner on the way.

Goldsteins was one of those outback shops that sells just about anything you don't want or need. They have a variety of knives with rusty blades, doilies no-one needs, bent knitting needles and very cheap clothes that most of the population wouldn't be seen dead in. Well, in actual fact Mr Goldstein did a big trade in clothes that people would be seen dead in. I mean, who wants to shell out for a new suit or dress when it's only going … well, you get the gist.

Blue pushed the door open and the bell tinkled. Mr Goldstein popped up from behind the counter and rubbed his hands together.

'Yes.'

'Um, I'm Bluey. Ya got a suit for me or someit.' Blue swallowed hard. He was way out of his comfort zone.

'No.' Mr Goldstein frowned.

'Gloria, she kinda said it was 'ere.'

'Gloria, Gloria.' Mr Goldstein rubbed his chin. 'Ah.' Light dawned, although it was only a slither at this point.

'You are the gentleman for the suit.'

'That's it.'

'Yes, we are getting married today.' Hakim added for clarity.

'Are you now.' Goldstein looked the odd couple over. They had the hallmarks of 'couple' written all over them. Matching polo shirts will do that.

'An' I got a suit all picked out.'

'Have you now.'

'Yeah.'

'Me name's um, me name's Gaylore, Meredith Gaylore.' Bluey winced as he said it.

'Meredith is it.'

'Yeah. An' you wanna make sommit of it, you'll be answerin' to this,' Blue made a fist and held it high.

'Ok, Ok.' Mr Goldstein backed away. 'I'll just get it.'

'Ya shittin' me.' Blue looked at the powder blue suit. The powder blue *safari* suit.

'Anything wrong?'

Bluey didn't know where to start. He tipped back his hat and scratched his forehead.

'It's paid for.' Goldstein smoothed down the suit in the plastic wrapper.

'You want it, it's yours.'

Bluey thought it over. Gloria had picked it out. She had paid for it. She was expecting him to wear it. And somewhere deep-down Blue found a lose thread of love and his heart stitched it in.

'I'll take it.'

'Bloody hell.' Bluey sat down in the sunken lounge and held his head in his hands. In all the kerfuffle he hadn't had time to think of a ring.

'She'll kill me for sure.'

'Ya not married yet, just wait Blue,' Lance looked over to Gwen and blew her a kiss.

'What'll I do?'

'Ya need to get sommit pronto.'

'Yeah, that's it.' Blue jumped up. He ran around in a circle and sat down.

'Now listen Bluey,' Lance grabbed his arm. 'Don't panic.'

'I have a ring.' Hakim pulled the ring off his finger. 'It is from Iran.'

'Nah. I can't take it.'

'What does it say Hakim?' Sylvia took the ring and looked at the Arabic inscription.

'I don't know.'

'I don't believe that?' Sylvia gave him a look.

'Well … It says …'

'Yes?'

'It says, my pin number. I can never remember, so I had it inscribed.' Hakim shrugged and smiled.

'Well, I think it says love conquers all.' Sylvia handed the ring to Bluey.

'Love conquers all,' Bluey said.

'I like it.' Rayleen agreed.

'Love conquers all.' Bluey gave the ring to Hakim. 'Ya gotta take care of it, and when the time comes, give it to me.'

'It's the duty of the best man,' Sylvia said.

'I can do this.'

'Sorted.' Rod sat back.

Gloria had always wanted to get married on a beach, somewhere exotic.

The Wollopi footy ground was the next best thing. It had two huge paperbark gum trees near the south end and public toilets in the car park.

The chairs had been set out in the shade of the morning, but by 2pm they were in full sun and to sit on them would be akin to torture.

Bluey's family hugged the slim slither of shade and passed the aeroguard around like it was the drug of choice.

'Skyla held her bouquet of wattle in limp hands and sagged against her uncle Darren.

'I'm dying here.' Someone had pulled a chair from the sun and given it to Agnes. It was too hot to sit on.

'The matrimonial agent wouldn't come out of her air-conditioned car until the bride arrived. They all gave her a withering stare as her car thrummed in tune with the insects.

'Blue, is she coming?' Hakim wiped his face with his shirt tail.

'I reckon.' Blue was beginning to leave large dark stains under his arms. The safari suit was tight, the belt had nylon backing which had as much absorbency as a new tea-towel, and it pricked.

They looked to the road in hope. And there in the distance was a car, then two, then four.

'Is that them?' Lance pointed.

'I dunno.' Bluey squinted and Ralph barked. Beaut joined in as the cars appoached.

'Bloody Nora, it's the mob.'

'Mob?' Sylvia asked.

'They are my abo friends.' Hakim squinted and watched the mob drive into town. He waved and they veered over to the footy field and stopped in a shower of dust.

'Bluey.' Chook bounded out of the car and gave Bluey a hug.

'Bluey,' Tommo followed. Then they saw Hakim.

'It's bloody Abdul.' There were back pats. Friendly shoves, man hugs all round, then the women tumbled out of the cars and began talking.

'I knew it was you.' Nellie kissed Hakim and slapped his bum.

'Hakim?' Sylvia thought she might exercise some territorial rights of her own.

'This is my sheila.'

Nellie looked Sylvia over and then gave her a hug. 'Ya got a good un there.' She slapped Hakim and laughed.

'We heard ya was getting hitched.'

'Bloody Nora.'

'Wouldn't miss it, would we Charlie?'

'Nah. Bluey's our mate eh?'

'Yeah.'

The family stood to one side wide eyed.

Jocko and Slim watched from the Bar & Grill over the road.

'This is gonna be good. Those blokes know how to party.'

'Ya got the stuff Blue?' Nellie nudged him.

'Stuff?'

'Yeah, me shoppin' and all that.' Nellie's three kids hung off her dress and looked expectant.

'Shoppin'?' The penny dropped and Blue nodded. It's in my ute.' Bluey pointed to the car park. Ralph ran about jumping and barking at the commotion and everyone missed the bride pulling up in the only thing resembling a stretch limo. The hearse was lined with flowers, and had a white ribbons from the bonnet.

Gloria was resplendent in a kaftan, that stalwart of the 1970's that hides a multitude of excesses and has as much style as a pop up tent. The Kaftan was adorned with diamantes around the neck and threw up a disco glitter ball of sparkles on the bride's face.

She stood on the footpath and adjusted herself when there was a strange sound in the sky.

Everyone looked up.

It's not every day a television chef helicopters into Wollopi with an entourage of hangers on. I could say agog, but even Wollopi can have too much of agog.

The crowd watched as the helicopter began to land and the dust flew in all directions. Lance hung onto his comb-over with determination.

Maylee practically threw herself down the front steps of the B & G and broke into a sprint to greet her guest. Crispin and Rupert were of a more sedate pace, but not far behind.

Giles Malthorpe stepped from the helicopter and waved. Crispin waved back

Agnes lost the facility of speech. She pointed and looked like a fish gasping for air.

'Mum?' Gwen made her mother sit down.

'It's …' Agnes swallowed the dust and formed the words.

'It's Giles Malthorpe.'

'So it is.' Sylvia shaded her eyes and watched as Giles air kissed Crispin and threw back his head and laughed.

'It's Giles Malthorpe,' Agnes said again. She rose from her seat and started to make her way to the middle of the footy field, her eye fixed on the celeb.

'Mum, the wedding.' Gwen held her back.

'It's Giles.' Agnes popped her eyeballs back into their sockets and sat down.

Jocko sniffed and watched,

'Beats me why some people go all crazy for some bloke on the tele. I'll never understand it. One of life's impondribbles.'

'Yeah.' Slim scratched his head. 'It's bloody impond a'right.' His conjugation a touch of genius.

Gloria gathered her kaftan around her legs and walked over the dirt carpark to the shade of the trees. The wind had knocked most of her hair sideways.

'Oh dear,' Rupert whipped out a comb and tried to attend to repairs when Giles and Crispin, arm in arm toddled over.

Agnes genuflected.

'Mum, get up.' Gwen pulled her up.

'Now Giles, listen.' Crispin began, 'It's just about the most darling wedding you've ever been to. Here's Bluey, and Gloria. They're just gorgeous.' Bluey and Gloria were

250

thrust in front of the celeb. Bluey pulled at his belt and Gloria grabbed her wayward kaftan in one hand and held out the other.

'Charming.' Giles looked at the hand.

'Maylee hovered and listened in.

It was when the camera's arrived and Giles mentioned something about a live feed that everyone turned into planks of wood.

Gloria opened and shut her mouth. Bluey began to sweat and forgot to blink. Sylvia looked like she had a goal post up her back and Agnes fainted.

The wedding celebrant popped up mid introduction.

'I've got a funeral at 3 you know. I can't keep 'em waiting.' When, in fact, the deceased had all the time in the world, and later it would be remarked upon that ol' Duncan Waters *was,* after all, late for his own funeral.

Gloria gave the officious woman a stare worthy of 35 years behind the bar. It was enough to get the proceedings going.

A bush wedding is nothing like a city wedding. There are the flies, the dust, the camera crew and beer. It's a winning combination.

Felicity Humphries took on a solemn air as she officiated, looking at her watch several times.

When it came time for the vows, Bluey swallowed hard.

'Do you, Meredith, Francis Gaylore …' There was a snicker at the back. Gloria turned and narrowed her eyes.

Ralph barked and Skyla fainted in the heat. Rayleen pulled her into the shade and revived her with some ice from Nellie's esky.

'Oh, bloody hell, Of course I do.' Bluey looked at Gloria and grinned.

'And do you Gloria Therese Gerkoff …'

'Yes, yes, yes.' Gloria squeezed Bluey's hand.

Hakim came forward and pulled the ring from his pocket.

'Oh, Blue,' Gloria grabbed that sucker and slipped it on her finger before Blue had time to blink.

'What does it say Bluey?' Gloria looked at the ring.

In the heat of the moment Bluey couldn't remember. He looked to his relatives. They mouthed, love conquers all. Hakim leaned over and whispered, 'love conquers all.'

'Thanks mate.' Blue took a breath.

'Love conquers all.' Blue said as if he had thought of it himself.

There was a cheer and before the ink was dry the whole gaggle had retreated to the Peninsular Bar & Grill, the camera men leading the charge.

'Meredith eh?' Jocko jabbed Slim.

'That's a girl's name init?'

'It's my husband's name so shut ya gob.' If Gloria had wedding nerves, they had abated, somewhat.

'WhadIsay?' Slim ducked, just in case.

Agnes sycophanted herself to Giles as he worked the crowd for the cameras. His minions had set up in the Bar & Grill's kitchen and were cooking up a storm. Maylee flitted, hovered and fluttered.

It took a minute of two for the crowd to slake their thirst before Skyla attracted the attention of her mother and pointed.

'Look mum, we're on the tele.'

And such is the nature of television, people would rather watch it, than real life.

'Oh, look, there's Bluey.' Nellie nudged Roger who was standing next to Blue.

The crowd look on as Giles smiled for the audience, Agnes strapped to his trouser leg.

The wedding guests were herded into the ladies lounge and Giles, Rupert and Crispin took charge of seating arrangements.

Bluey and Gloria were plonked at the top table near the dart board and told to stay.

The tables were squashed together for everyone else and those that couldn't fit stood in the doorway.

Giles held up his hand for quiet. A hush fell over the audience.

'Now, we're on a commercial break. When the red light comes back on, just relax, smile and have a good time. Giles turned to Crispin, 'this is pure gold, I'm telling you, I've got a gong on this one for sure.'

'Oh, Ruppee and I just knew you'd like it.' Crispin pulled a errant wisp of hair from Giles's style and put it back in place.

The red light blinked and it might have been a timber merchant's yard. Planks of wood sat about trying to act natural.

Giles clapped his hands and the wood pile jumped.

'Speech, speech.' Crispin tried to jolly the mood along.

'Bloody Nora,' Bluey wiped the sweat from his face and stood up.

He cleared his throat.

'Thanks for commin''

The crowd clapped. 'Um …' The crowd waited. 'Um, I'd like ta say, I'm a lucky man.' There was a small cheer.

'Gloria's a good sort.' Blue was getting into his stride. This pronouncement elicited another cheer.

'An' a good cook too.' He looked at Giles and grinned.

'She's a bloody rippa.' He sat down and mopped his brow with a serviette. The paper stuck to his face and made him look like an accident victim from a slip on peppbledash.

Hakim stood up and held his hand for quiet.

'I am the best man. He is my best friend in Straya. He is my mate. I am very happy to know Bluey. He is bloody rippa.'

Giles gave his cameraman a high five. He had hit pay-dirt.

The food arrived as fast as the beer. The nuance of gumleaf piquancy to tender duck strips and bottlebrush steak mince was lost after the first keg change. Fish with seaweed soufflé was eaten with Maylee's spring rolls and the wild peach melba with native vanilla sorbet was washed down with cold beer. It was all just perfect, as Gloria said after cutting the cake that looked like a lamington that had been out in the sun too long.

Blue managed to dispose of his leftovers into a napkin.

'What's that luv?' Gloria felt the bulge in his pocket.

'It's … it's … for Ralph. Best mate I've ever had.' Gloria wrapped a spring roll and put it in her kaftan pocket and winked.

'Jeez, you're bloody t'rrific.' He looked at the small portions on his plate,

'Your grubs better than this lot.'

'Oh. Blue.' Gloria kissed her new man.

'This'll put Wollopi on the map.' Jocko looked at the big screen.'

'Ya mean to tell me that we're not even on a map?' Slim picked a spring roll from a plate as it went back to the kitchen.

'Ya not the dumbest person on the planet Slim, but ya sure better hope he doesn't die.'

'Who?'

'I am glad I didn't go to New Bloody Zealand. This is a very happy day,' Hakim said as he drew Sylvia to his side.

'It's great.' Sylvia sipped her beer.

'You like beer?'

"course.'

'Me too.' Hakim ordered two more.

'You like dogs?'

"course.'

'You like to marry me?'

Sylvia ran her hands through her hair and jangled her bangles.

'Oh, Hakim.'

'Bloody rippa.'

'Bluey, I am getting married.' Hakim shouted Bluey a beer. 'You will be my best man?'

'Mate.'

'Mate.'

Colloquially speaking.

For those that need a handle on the Aussie lingo.
(for those that need a helping hand on the Aussie language.)

6 o'clock swill: For 50 years up until 1967 pubs closed at 6pm. Drinkers had to get all they wanted by 6pm and it was a bit of a push to get it down your neck before closing time.

Arvo: afternoon

Biffo: fight

Big smoke: the big city, or anything bigger than where you come from.

Black top: bitumen road.

Bleed the lizard: men take a piss.

Blower: on the blower, the telephone.

Cacked himself: cacked himself laughing. Soiled his pants laughing although it is just a saying and not literal

Choke a darkie: doing a poo. Made famous by Barry Humphries (Dame Edna)

Chook: Chicken, usually a cooked chook.

Choppers: teeth.

Clobber: clothes.

Copped an eyeful: given a good look.

Crook: sick.

Daks: men's underpants.

Dead horse: tomato sauce

Dekkie: a look

Dinkum: the real truth

Drongo: idiot
Duds: clothes, usually the good ones for an occasion.
Dump: poo
Dunny: toilet, usually the outside one
Flagon of steam: flagon of drink, usually sherry
Hitched: married
Jocks: men's underpants
Jubes: lollies with gelatine, very chewy
Kelpie: Australian cattle dog breed
Lingo: language
Lollie: sweets
Mullet: hair cut long at the back and short on top
Mozzie: mosquito
NAIDOC: a week when the indigenous population celebrate their unique place in Australia. National Aborigines and Islanders Day Observance Committee.
Nuddy: nude
Pan licker: dog
Radio rentals: a shop that rents all your household needs.
Reffo: refugee
Rippa: terrific
Ringer: outback worker on a cattle station
Road train: a truck with more than one trailer
Roo: kangaroo
Rooted: broken, finished off, tired
Schooner: large glass of beer
Shonky: something a bit suspect
Shout: paying for someone else
Slash: piss
Smoko: taking a break from work
Straya: Australia
Strewth: exclamation of a fact
Strides: trousers
Stubbies: work shorts

Stunned mullets: surprised look
Tucker: food
Ute: utility truck with a cab for 2 and a tray at the back
Yakka: work
Zebra suntan: getting a striped tan in prison

Pierogi: filled dumplings made by wrapping unleavened dough around savoury or sweet filling and cooked in boiling water. An Eastern European dish.